THE ART OF
THE
BATMAN

DC

WRITTEN BY **JAMES FIELD**

FOREWORD BY **MATT REEVES**

BATMAN CREATED BY BOB KANE WITH BILL FINGER

ABRAMS, NEW YORK

CONTENTS

FOREWORD

When I was three years old, I had a fever. It was so high my parents had to feed me water through an eye-dropper just to keep me hydrated. As my temperature soared, a figure appeared on my ceiling . . . *Batman*. The Batmobile was up there, too. But I wasn't afraid. I knew he was protecting me. I was first introduced to Batman in the 1966 Adam West series. I didn't see any of the campy irony of that show. I just saw The Caped Crusader, fighting for justice. I was captivated by his theatricality. His suit. His car. His gadgets. Batman was special.

The story of Batman has thrived in various forms for more than eighty years. It has great mythic underpinnings. But truth is, Batman isn't really a Super Hero.

He doesn't have a superpower. What he has is an incredible drive to make *meaning* of his life. I've always experienced that meaning in going to the movies. We live in a world of highs and lows and tremendous chaos, yet we can go to the movies and experience a story that reflects and makes sense of the world around us. I find my drive and meaning in the process of filmmaking. To put myself in the shoes of a character who I am not, and to find a commonality between who I am and who that character is, and to understand the world through that character's eyes.

There have been a number of great Batman movies. The challenge for us was how to do another and make it feel warranted. I set a course for us to be very ambitious, and everyone involved gave it their all. One of the exciting (and terrifying) aspects about creating a Batman film is there's no way to take it on and *just* make a Batman film—you set out to make a *definitive* Batman film. From James Chinlund's production design, Greig Fraser's photography, and Dan Lemmon's visual effects to Jacqueline Durran's costumes, Glyn Dillon and David Crossman's Batsuit, and what Ash Thorp helped us achieve with the Batmobile—each of these elements came together by everyone pushing to their limits to be and do their best, which in a way, is a very Batman concept. And we were pushing at a very difficult time, because while we were making this film, the world itself was going through great confusion and trauma. Having this story to focus on was a gift for all of us.

Ever since I was a kid and aspiring filmmaker, I've always found it exhilarating to see other people go through the creative process. I can never get enough of looking behind the scenes and seeing how all aspects of a film are achieved. The number of people required to realize the scale and level of detail of *The Batman* is astonishing, and here, you can take a walk with us down the various paths of how the concepts were born. In this book you won't see our doubts, but I think you should know that we had all those doubts to arrive, finally, at *The Batman*. I hope revealing a little of our process may touch and inspire some of you who are interested in the same thing we are. The drive to find meaning through art. Looking back on it now, it all feels a bit like a fever dream. The Batman from my ceiling now flickers on the big screen.

MATT REEVES

CONCEPT ART

INTRODUCTION

"What I wanted to do was to take Batman and have him solve a mystery in what would not be an origin tale for him, but instead would refer to his origins, and ultimately shake him to his very core," began *The Batman* director Matt Reeves. "You could have it be very, very practical and grounded, and totally thrilling. But I also thought it could be extremely psychological, and the most emotional Batman movie yet." Back in 2007, the groundbreaking viral marketing campaign for Reeves' "found-footage" monster film *Cloverfield* encouraged eager audiences to piece together the film's secret story, and in the movie itself they would follow its characters as they start to unpack the mystery behind their city's destruction (spoiler: a gigantic monster attack). Ten years later, the director would begin a journey that invited cinemagoers to solve a mystery along with The World's Greatest Detective: Batman.

Batman's long-standing reputation as The World's Greatest Detective can be traced all the way back to *Detective Comics* #27 (1939). The issue embroiled readers in "The Case of the Chemical Syndicate," introducing them to its exciting new mystery-solving, crime-fighting protagonist, "The Bat-Man." The character was immediately described as a "mysterious and adventurous figure, fighting for righteousness and apprehending the wrong doer, in his lone battle against the evil forces of society," which has largely remained at the core of Batman—as has his aptitude for sleuthing. *Batman: The Animated Series*, which ran from 1992 to 1995, not only wowed audiences with exciting action and genuinely emotional character arcs but also showed viewers a Batman who undertook investigative work, giving airtime to show his intricate thought process as a detective. The 1996 Jeph Loeb/Tim Sale comics series *The Long Halloween* has long been hailed as a seminal piece of Batman storytelling; in it, The Dark Knight uncovers a dark and twisted murder plot that weaves together the lives of Gotham City's most prominent figures on both sides of the coin. Gamers have also had the chance to experience mystery-solving as Batman firsthand in the highly acclaimed *Arkham* video games, as puzzle-solving was placed front and center as both narrative and gameplay devices. However, Batman's detective work has never been placed front and center in any of the character's cinematic outings—a key building block that would

CONCEPT SKETCH

distinguish *The Batman* from other incarnations of The Dark Knight. "He started as The World's Greatest Detective," said Reeves, "and that has been touched on lightly in the movies, but it's never been a full-blown mystery and detective story. I thought that there would be a way."

Reeves would then reunite with producer Dylan Clark, the team behind the films *Dawn of the Planet of the Apes* and *War for the Planet of the Apes*. Together they understood the challenge of bringing something new to the table. "When you come into eighty years of Batman lore, it's humbling. You have to ask yourself: Are you up to the task of doing something great for the canon of the Batman movies and for the fans?" wondered Clark. "There's an excitement working on Batman. There is a terror working on Batman. You know, it's just one of those things, like the level of care, precision, focus. You just want this movie and this experience to be the best possible thing for an audience."

Perhaps a film with Batman as The World's Greatest Detective was waiting for a fittingly forensic approach. "Matt is a very meticulous director," said Greig Fraser, the film's director of photography. Having worked with Reeves back in 2009 on *Let Me In*, Fraser knew that he was the right man for the job. "There's a lot of similarities between him and The Batman in that sense, in that they're both very meticulous characters and very meticulous people." The parallels between the natures of Batman and Reeves wouldn't stop there, with the movie's lead actor, Robert Pattinson, suggesting a deeper connection. "There's a lot of different aspects which cross over with Bruce's mind. He's definitely obsessive, he's incredibly patient about things, but it's like watching a conductor of a really good orchestra," recalled Pattinson. "He'll get hyper focused on tiny, little actions, but he seems to be able to keep the entire story in a macro view in his mind the entire time." Another trusted collaborator asked to join the project was production designer James Chinlund, following Chinlund's acclaimed work with Reeves on the *Apes* movies. "He is one of the most specific directors I've ever met in terms of the fact that, first of all, he's writing every word—which is a huge advantage," said Chinlund of Reeves. "He's weaving the fabric of the movie, and what I find particularly amazing about him is that the fabric is woven so tightly that if you try and remove one thread from the fabric he's created, the whole thing doesn't work." Chinlund continued, "This web of clues and this whole detective story are

so interwoven that it's been an incredible process working together trying to create this world that, not only in the sets, but the props and the graphics, the computer graphics, every detail is actually so critical in terms of supporting and scaffolding this narrative and detective story and making it all work."

With a wealth of source material to draw on, the filmmakers looked back at some of Batman's most iconic detective stories for inspiration. Reeves didn't need to look too far, as his screenwriting teacher at the University of Southern California was none other than *The Long Halloween* writer Jeph Loeb—the very same person who, years before, had told Reeves that he should become a writer. However, *The Batman* wouldn't be a live-action adaptation of the story. "While we're not doing *The Long Halloween*," said Reeves, "the idea that we're doing a serial-killer story that is also a story about Batman where we go on a personal journey with him, that was very inspiring to me. That story and *Dark Victory* and *Hush* were really important in the beginning of all this, as was Darwyn Cooke's *Ego*, with its great psychological understanding of the character." Additionally, Reeves and his team would turn to the Frank Miller/David Mazzucchelli classic, *Year One*. "Something as iconic and simple as grounding it the way that *Year One* does was a revelation," said Reeves. For Greig Fraser, it provided a launch pad for their story—hailing *Year One* as "very intimate, very detailed. This film is very similar, where every story piece, every story beat, every frame, everything that happens in this film. Nothing happens in this film by accident. Everything has a story."

JAMES FIELD

CONCEPT ART

MILLER HARBOR

Old Gotham

Grant Park

GRANT PARK

Anchorage

Gotham Village

JONES PARK

Jones Park

Neville Street

Arena

City Hall

Financial District

Stock Exchange

Englehart

Gotham Square

DOWNTOWN

Chinatown

Theatre Row

West Harlow

Little Odessa

Cathedral Square

Vauxhall Center

Battergate

Clock Tower

COTTON PARK

Hinkley River

Atlantic Quays

North Docks

GOTHAM RIVER

HINKLEY RIVER

Tricorner

Tricorner Central

East Docklands

West Docks

Tricorner Yards

N
W — E
S

GOTHAM CITY ISLANDS

Gotham River

N
W — E
S

Uptown

Sprang River

Midtown

Downtown Island

Miller Harbor

114

DOWNTOWN

Hinkley River

Tricorner

Stats:
Population
4,912,032

Area (Approx.):
34km²

0   1 km
0   1 mile

22101/V04

Map of

Gotham City Downtown

REGIONAL MAP

SCALES
APPROXIMATE

0   1 km
0   1 mile

H	Hospitals
S	Subway Stations
—	Subway Line
—	Streets/Highways
•	Main Public Schools
▬	Downtown Boundary

WHO'S WHO

CHARACTERS

ANDY SERKIS
Alfred

COLIN FARRELL
Oz/The Penguin

JAYME LAWSON
Bella Reál

JEFFREY WRIGHT
Lieutenant James Gordon

JOHN TURTURRO
Carmine Falcone

PAUL DANO
The Riddler

PETER SARSGAARD
District Attorney
Gil Colson

ROBERT PATTINSON
Bruce Wayne/
The Batman

ZOË KRAVITZ
Selina Kyle

CREATIVE TEAM

ALEX POTTS
Previs Artist

DAN LEMMON
VFX Supervisor

DAVID CROSSMAN
Costume Designer:
The Batsuit

DOMINIC TUOHY
SFX Supervisor

DYLAN CLARK
Producer

FAE CORRIGAN
Virtual Reality Illustrator

GLYN DILLON
Costume Designer &
Chief Concept Artist:
The Batsuit

GRANT ARMSTRONG
Supervising Art Director

GREIG FRASER
Director of Photography

JACQUELINE DURRAN
Costume Designer

JAMES CHINLUND
Production Designer

JAMIE WILKINSON
Props & Weapons Master

JOSEPH HIURA
Art Director

LAURA DISHINGTON
Lead Graphic Designer

MARK ROCCA
Head of Department,
Prop Making

MATT REEVES
Director

MIKE FONTAINE
Prosthetic Artist

MIKE MARINO
Prosthetic Makeup
Designer

NAOMI DONNE
Makeup Designer

PIERRE BOHANNA
Supervising Costume
Effects Modeler

ROBERT ALONZO
Supervising Stunt
Coordinator

TAD DAVIS
Art Director

ZOE TAHIR
Hair Designer

CONCEPT ART

CONCEPT ART

VENGEANCE
THE BATMAN

The Batman is not an origin story, that much is clear—at least not for Batman, anyway. "We've seen lots of origin stories," remarked director Matt Reeves. "And I thought, 'I don't want to do another origin story.' I want to have Batman be along an arc of *becoming*, because to me the danger with Super Heroes is once they have perfected their methods, they can turn into ciphers. It's like, 'Oh, well the character just represents the pursuit of goodness.' Whereas our Batman has a lot of room to improve. He has to push harder, evolve, strive to become better. And the journey of this story ends up being a huge awakening for him.'"

In *The Batman*, we meet a Bruce Wayne who is in his second year of operation as the vigilante Batman, working on his own and with his own resources. "He's designed his Batsuit, he's designed his own Batmobile. He doesn't have Lucius Fox there to help him," said Dylan Clark, the film's producer. "What we liked was the opportunity to say, 'Here is an obsessed person who is vengeance personified, who is wanting to put himself in this situation where he can endure everything that you have to endure in order to fight crime in the city.'" Vengeance is at the very heart of this Batman. In addition to "Vengeance" being chosen as the film's production code name, vengeance itself is a core motivation for Bruce's vigilantism and what he intends to personify when wearing the Batsuit. "The great thing about Batman," mused Matt Reeves, "it's such a psychological story. And so, this whole idea of the emotional pursuit of what he's after and what he's willing to do to get there, and how he turns into his shadow self—that sort of complexity, I think, is really unique to Batman."

"At the end of the day, what I wanted was a Batman who was exceedingly human. I wanted you to see this guy who does these amazing things, but in a way, his scars are his biggest strength. What happened to him made him perfectly suited to be the person who will push himself to any length, because it's the only way he can make meaning out of his life," Reeves continued. Bringing this emotionally complex Bruce Wayne to life required an actor who could wear the psychological transformation both internally and externally. In 2018, Clark met with Robert Pattinson: "We weren't meeting about anything in particular, and then we just started talking about Batman at the end of the meeting," remembered Pattinson. "I had never been interested in a Super Hero movie. It'd never been in my periphery at all. And for some reason, Batman just always stood out as a kind of very special, separate entity. It's always the way the movies have been made and where the character sits in the kind of cultural lexicon. It always feels very individual, and it holds a lot of totemic importance." With scriptwriting still under way, Pattinson met with Reeves, who took the actor through some of the early storyboards. "It sounded quite radically different from anything we'd seen in Batman movies before," said Pattinson. "And it reignited my enthusiasm even more."

Having charmed the broadest of audiences early on in his career with cinematic adaptations of the *Harry Potter* and *Twilight* novels, Pattinson spent much of the 2010s wowing cinemagoers with his critically acclaimed character work, collaborating with a roster of award-winning directors that includes David Cronenberg (*Cosmopolis*, *Map to the Stars*), James Gray (*The Lost City of Z*), Josh and Benny Safdie (*Good Time*), Claire Denis (*High Life*), and Robert Eggers (*The Lighthouse*), to name but a few. "I think he's got the right amount of mystery and emotion and angst and rage and all of those things," said Zoë Kravitz, the actress who joins Pattinson's Batman as Selina Kyle. "We're meeting Batman in such a specific time, a very emotional time, and I think Rob is not only capable, but delighted to go into those weird dark corners of Bruce

58%

~~JULIA~~
Janice

MAZZUCCHELLI

Wayne." Rather importantly for the role of Batman, and for an actor being eyed for the Batsuit, he had something else going for him. "He certainly has a really excellent jaw," remarked actor Peter Sarsgaard, "which I think every Batman needs because you're going to be seeing a lot of it." Pattinson's Batman screen test seemed to place a real emphasis on the *test* aspect. Following in the footsteps of the likes of Adam West, Michael Keaton, Val Kilmer, George Clooney, Christian Bale, and Ben Affleck is no easy task—neither is having to put on one of their suits. "I was just starting Christopher Nolan's movie *Tenet*, which I was also terrified about," recalled Pattinson. The *Batman Forever* Batsuit was used during the actor's screen test, which had an immediate effect on Pattinson."I was saying to Dylan and Matt, 'Wow, it is very transformative,' and he's [Dylan's] like, 'Yeah, you're dressed as Batman. It should feel transformative.'"

Joining a long legacy of actors and directors who have been at the helm of Batman meant that, for Pattinson and Reeves, there was a very real requirement to realize what would define this particular performance. "It both increases the pressure on you, and shows that there are lots of different angles to the character, "said Pattinson. "It's almost that the more people reinterpret it, the space to reinvent it gets

smaller, but I think it actually just gets more specific and I find that really fun, to try and find just a new way of doing something when a lot of your heroes have played it before, and try to find a new angle on it." Pattinson continued, "He doesn't necessarily know that he's gonna save the day, and I think that's an important differentiation of this Batman. Basically, the options are death or being Batman. I don't know if it's hopelessness, but there's a desperation to it which is a little bit different."

A Batman who's still discovering his potential (along with his limits) and doesn't have the industry and expertise of Wayne Industries for sophisticated, expensive gadget development means that the vigilante is reliant on a certain type of brutal, untethered punishment. Enter Robert Alonzo, supervising stunt coordinator (*Once Upon a Time . . . in Hollywood, Jack Reacher, Star Trek* [2009]). With a compact training schedule, Alonzo would work with Pattinson to create a fighting style that not only appeared reactive and relentless but embodied the physical and psychologically transformative qualities of putting on the Batsuit. "All the fights seem very personal," said Pattinson. "I think in a way, he's imagining that these are the people who killed his parents, like every single one of them. He's not just disarming people—it's punishing them."

I think all Batman fans will have their own idea as to what is the ideal ear length or ear height, and I'm quite pleased to say that I was along with Matt Reeves. I kind of like slightly higher ones. It's not too high and it's not too short. It feels like Batman, to me.

GLYN DILLON

THE BATSUIT

In addition to the distinct performative elements, there was a requirement to establish a look and feel that was unique to *The Batman*. With a character so intrinsically linked with darkness, it was a case of creating a visual identity that utilized dark cinematography without compromising on the film's watchability. "We wanted to remind viewers about the early comic books, the early silhouettes, the shapes, the character that lurks in the shadows," realized Greig Fraser, director of photography. "We wanted to create something that was very easily recognizable."

The creation of a Batsuit that reflects almost a century of iconography, let alone bringing something new and exciting to the table, was no easy feat. Following their work together on *Solo: A Star Wars Story*, costume designers David Crossman and Glyn Dillon were brought on board to take on the challenge. "One of the inspirations while I was writing was reading Lee Bermejo's *Batman Damned*, and in it he had a strikingly tactical-looking suit," recounted Matt Reeves. "It looked militaristic, almost like riot police gear." As with many of the film's aspects, a grounded approach was required when it came to designing the Batsuit. This needed to be a tactical, protective suit that could theoretically be built and pieced together by a young Bruce Wayne (in reality, the suit was pieced together by supervising costume effects modeler Pierre Bohanna and his team). "It wasn't an origin story, so you weren't seeing him making the Batsuit, but you were seeing what would be more of a prototype Batsuit," continued Reeves. "Something that could evolve over time, as he's only in year two of this grand criminological experiment that he is conducting to see if he can have an effect on crime in Gotham."

In terms of movie production practicalities, the costume first and foremost had to look the part. "Everything the costume team made the Batsuit from was beautifully textural, and reflected light in such an interesting, unique way," recalled Greig Fraser. "Every time I put a light on it, it sung." Photographing such a dark costume, with dark makeup around the eyes, had its own issues—as Fraser continued, "Trying to see into a character through a dark costume, through dark eyes, is very hard, because to illuminate that well enough to see emotion, but not give away the

mood, it's a fine balance. So, during the camera test it became quite clear that we really needed to fill light in the eyes, or not fill light in the eyes. If you watch *The Godfather*, there were times where they deliberately allowed Marlon Brando's eyes to go dark, because not seeing into the soul of a character is sometimes more telling than seeing into the soul of a character. So, finding that balance between seeing detail and not seeing detail was one of the big things that we explored very early on." Secondly, the Batsuit had to move properly—light, flexible materials for the extensive stunt work, and a comfortable enough daily wear for Robert Pattinson. "I had been in the *Batman Forever* Batsuit and realized you are basically a statue in there," recalled Pattinson. "So, the first time I put on this Batsuit there's so much more maneuverability."

The Batman's Batsuit required a great deal of effort to transform a shiny new costume into a battle-worn suit of armor, as the filmmakers wanted audiences to believe that this was a Batman who had been fighting on the streets for the last two years. "It's got loads of scuffs and tears on it already, it doesn't feel so Super Hero-y," said Pattinson. "There's a bullet indentation in the cowl, and every little scar on it shows. I think it's just a reminder of Batman's fallibility. I mean, he is just a guy in a suit. The suit does not make him invincible. It's just a few panels of bulletproof armor and the rest of it is just how much Bruce believes in it and how much his adversaries are scared of it, but I like seeing the external wounds on it." In addition to the visible wear and tear on the cowl from Batman's scrapes (including a nose piece that, according to Glyn Dillon, "makes him feel tougher, almost like he's got a slightly broken nose," while also referencing the classic cowl worn by Adam West in the 1966 *Batman* television series), great care was taken to make this Batman feel as intimidating as possible. "We're just trying to make it [the cowl] look mean and menacing and in a different way to how it's been done before in previous Batman films," remarked Dillon. "More demonic. And this is a little bit more skull-like."

The Batsuit's transformative qualities went beyond the physical, as wearing the costume itself became a powerful tool in becoming Batman. "You realize, quite quickly, the benefits of putting on the suit. You immediately feel incredibly powerful and ten times the size," Pattinson revealed. "There's so much history invested in the iconography, and so many people connect to it on such a deep level and for so many different reasons. You can feel that weight and responsibility, and it kind of bleeds into how Bruce feels about being Batman himself."

Matt (Reeves) wants everything to feel like it has a purpose, so with the suit we came up with this idea of it being a bit like a Russian pressure suit. The lacing detail up the side and back is based on what pilots would wear. And we've got elastic in the back so they can fight and stretch and punch freely.

It's not a real protective suit—but when we met with Robert Alonso, the head stunt coordinator, he was saying that it reminded him of an equestrian vest, which he said is one of the best protective vests a stuntman can wear because it's got similar kind of breaks in it, so that you've got a lot of mobility. And it's got pauldrons in the chest plate so, in theory, Batman will be protected from bullets and what have you.

GLYN DILLON

A lot of the paneling you see is very much taken from the ideas of ballistic shielding, etcetera, that is sewn into that. After the cowl, it looks like it's made from leather and stitched together, so the mechanical elements are very much built on top.

PIERRE BOHANNA

CONCEPT ART

CONCEPT ART

UNIT PHOTOGRAPHY

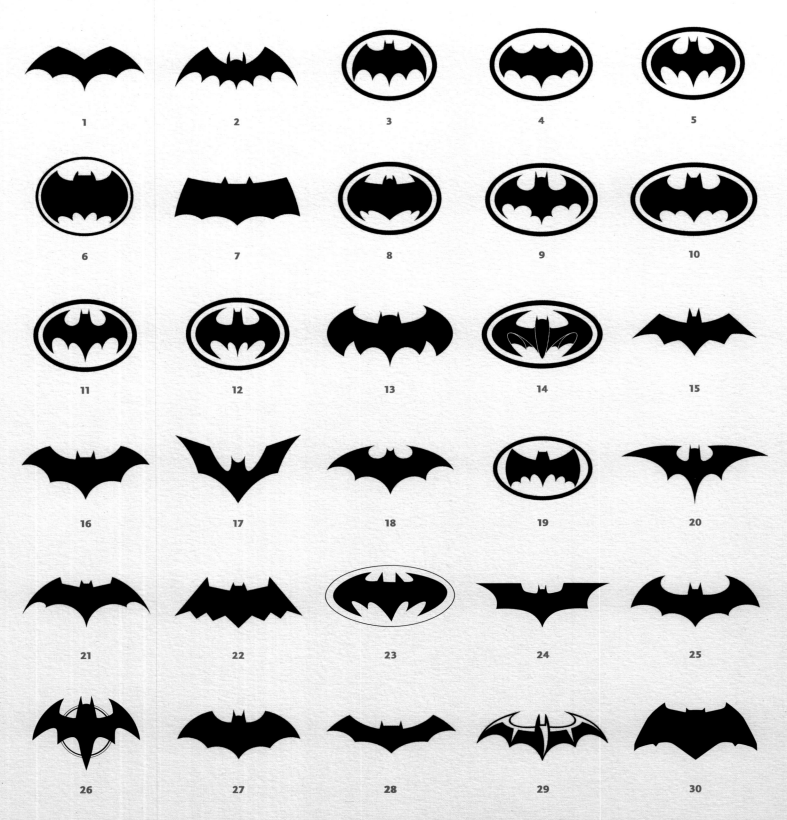

1 *Detective Comics #27* (comic book, first appearance), 1939; 2 *Detective Comics* (comic books), 1940s; 3 *Batman* (comic books), 1960s; 4 *Batman* (TV show), 1966; 5 *Batman* (comic books), 1970s; 6 *Batman: The Dark Knight Returns* (Book 1), 1986; 7 *Batman: The Dark Knight Returns* (Book 3), 1986; 8 *Batman* (comic books), 1980s; 9 *Batman* (movie), 1989; 10 *Batman: The Animated Series* (TV show), 1992; 11 *Batman Returns* (movie), 1992; 12 *Batman Forever* (movie), 1995; 13 *Batman: The Long Halloween* (comic book series), 1996; 14 *Batman & Robin* (movie), 1997; 15 *The New Batman Adventures* (animated series), 1997; 16 *Batman: War on Crime* (comic book), 1999; 17 *Batman Beyond* (animated series), 1999; 18 "Batman: Hush" (comic book storyline), 2002; 19 *The Batman* (animated series), 2004; 20 *Superman/Batman* (comic book), 2004; 21 *Batman Begins* (movie), 2005; 22 *All-Star Batman & Robin, the Boy Wonder* (comic book), 2005; 23 *Batman: The Brave and The Bold* (animated series), 2008; 24 *The Dark Knight* (movie), 2008, and *The Dark Knight Rises* (movie), 2012; 25 *Batman: Arkham Asylum* (video game), 2009; 26 *Flashpoint* (comic book series), 2011; 27 *Justice League* (DC New 52) #1 (comic book), 2011; 28 *Beware the Batman* (animated series), 2013; 29 DC animated movies, 2010s; 30 *Batman v Superman: Dawn of Justice* (movie), 2016

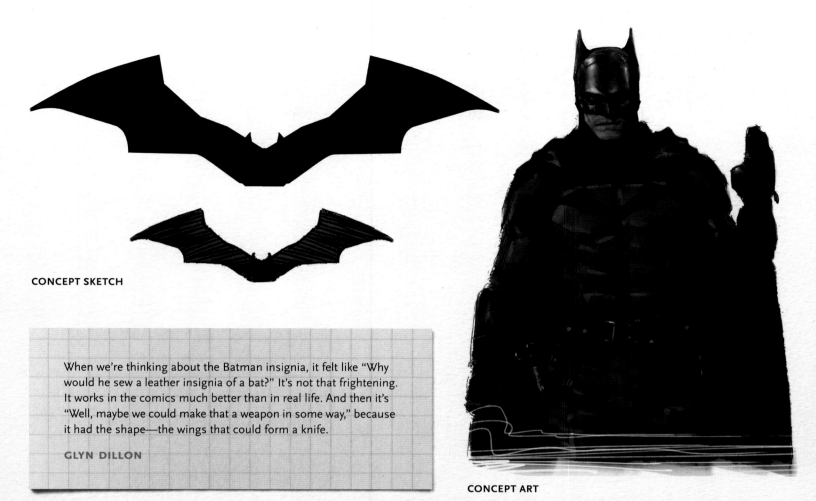

CONCEPT SKETCH

When we're thinking about the Batman insignia, it felt like "Why would he sew a leather insignia of a bat?" It's not that frightening. It works in the comics much better than in real life. And then it's "Well, maybe we could make that a weapon in some way," because it had the shape—the wings that could form a knife.

GLYN DILLON

CONCEPT ART

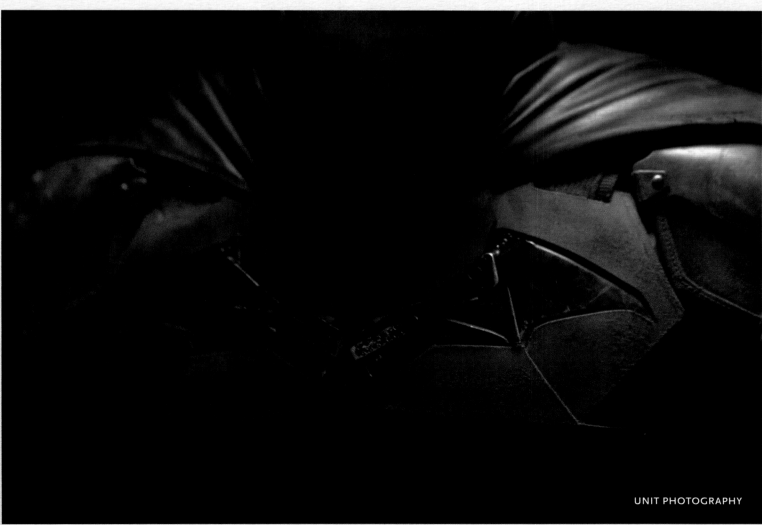

UNIT PHOTOGRAPHY

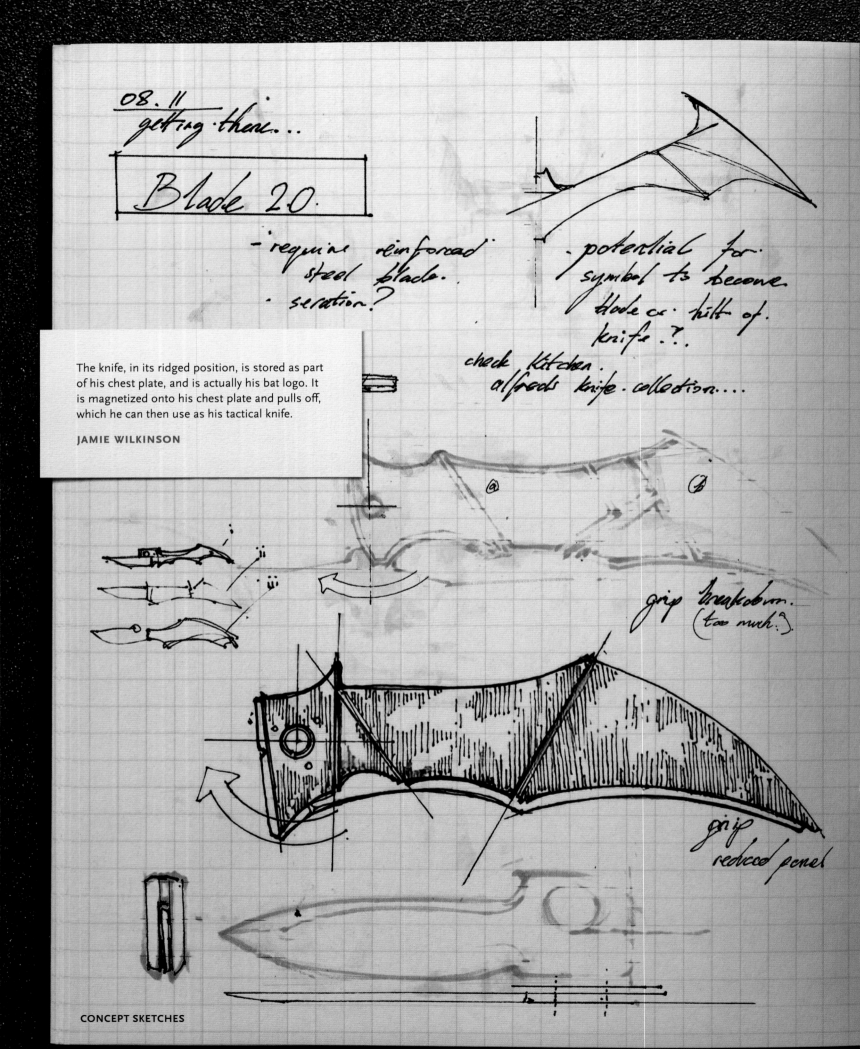

The knife, in its ridged position, is stored as part of his chest plate, and is actually his bat logo. It is magnetized onto his chest plate and pulls off, which he can then use as his tactical knife.

JAMIE WILKINSON

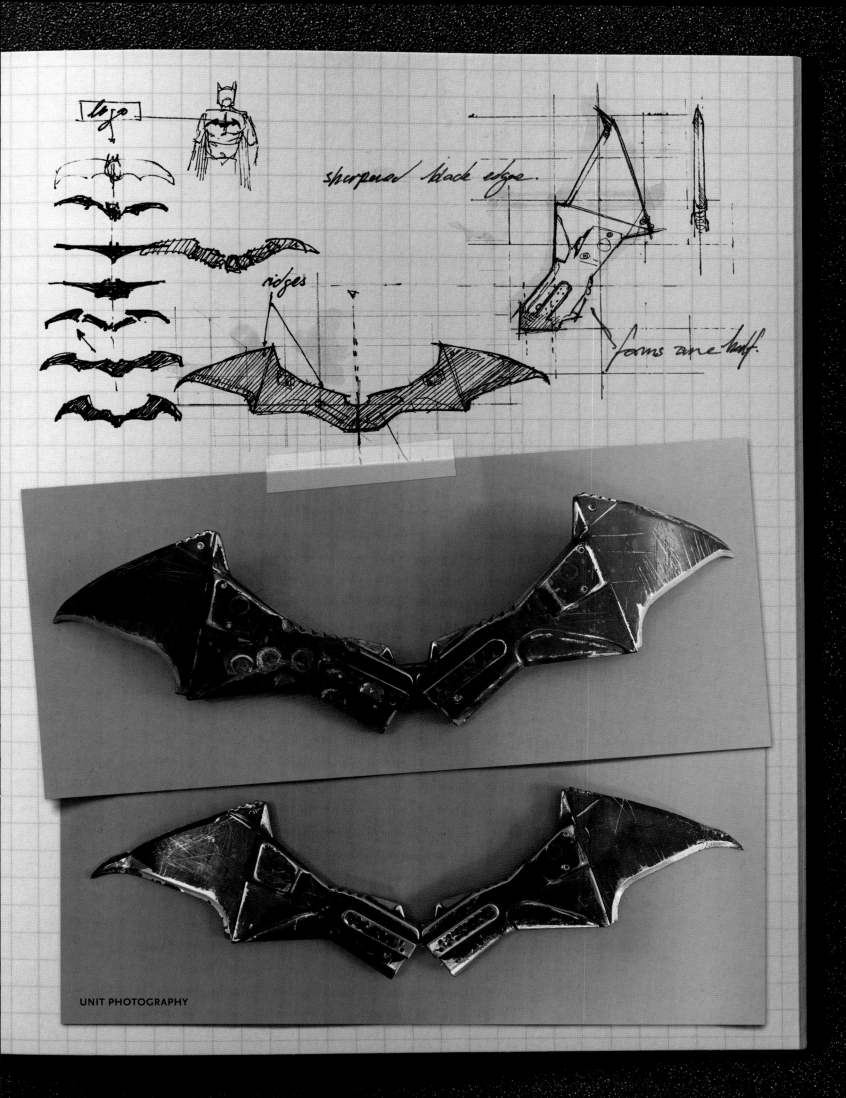

sharpened blade edge.

ridges

forms are half.

The idea of the Utility Belt—I thought it would be nice if he'd use stuff that you could get like from ex-military or police force. So instead of the kind of yellow or gold belt that they've had in the past, we've come to this very practical-looking, black leather, very realistic belt because it's from the real world.

With the neck of the cowl, we've done these pieces that are almost like vertebrae that will move when he moves his neck. That's the other thing we really wanted—for him to be able to move really well because, quite famously, the Tim Burton one couldn't. So we want him to be able to have that full motion.

GLYN DILLON

One of the very first drawings I did of the cowl, It had this kind of skull-like feel to it. It's indented, giving that shape that you have on a skull. And the eyes are quite skull-like. Matt wanted it to feel not like a rubberized thing. He wanted it to feel like Bruce Wayne has made it himself, so we were looking at it being leather, rather than previous Batman versions that've always been a rubber mold.

GLYN DILLON

UNIT PHOTOGRAPHY

TACTICAL WEAPONS

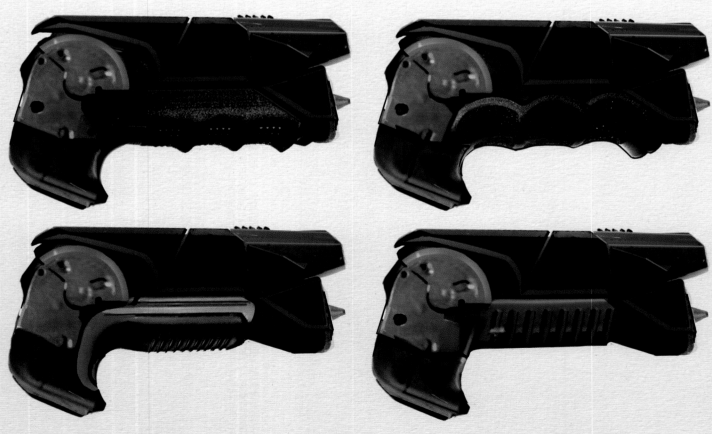

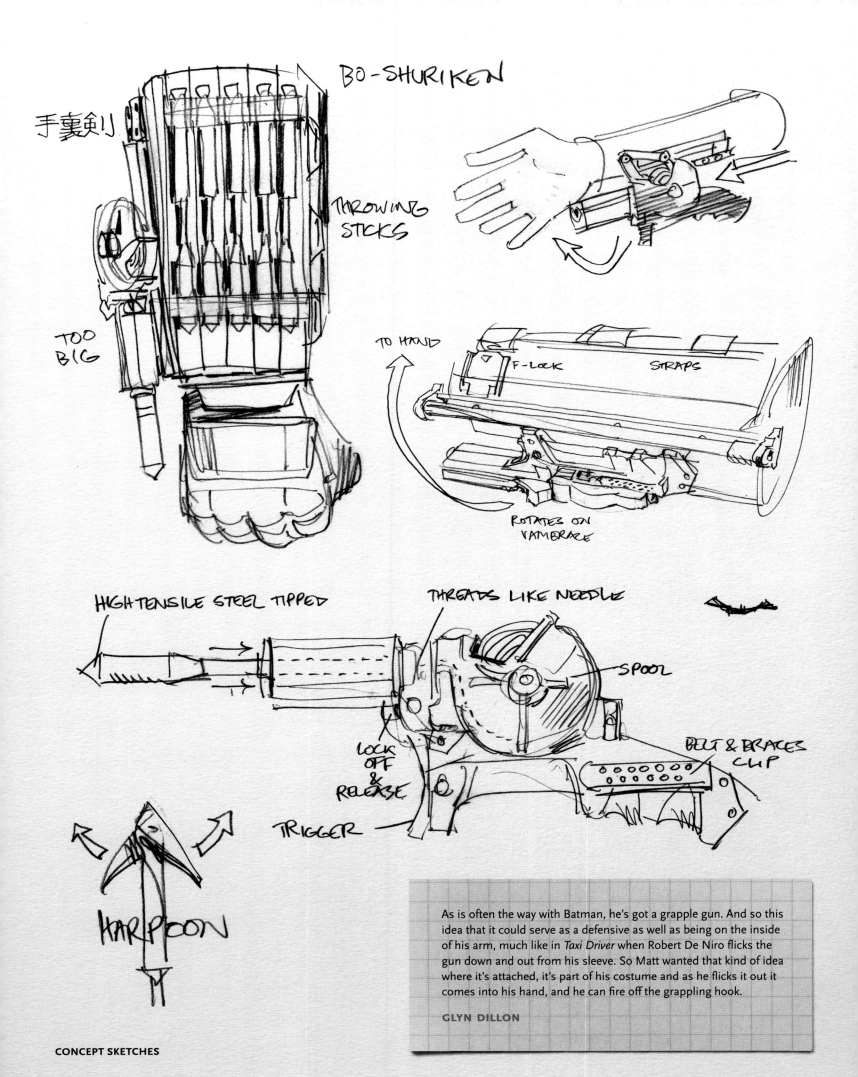

手裏剣

BO-SHURIKEN

THROWING STICKS

TOO BIG

TO HAND

F-LOCK   STRAPS

ROTATES ON VAMBRACE

HIGH TENSILE STEEL TIPPED

THREADS LIKE NEEDLE

SPOOL

LOCK OFF & RELEASE

BELT & BRACES CLIP

TRIGGER

HARPOON

As is often the way with Batman, he's got a grapple gun. And so this idea that it could serve as a defensive as well as being on the inside of his arm, much like in *Taxi Driver* when Robert De Niro flicks the gun down and out from his sleeve. So Matt wanted that kind of idea where it's attached, it's part of his costume and as he flicks it out it comes into his hand, and he can fire off the grappling hook.

GLYN DILLON

CONCEPT SKETCHES

CONCEPT ART

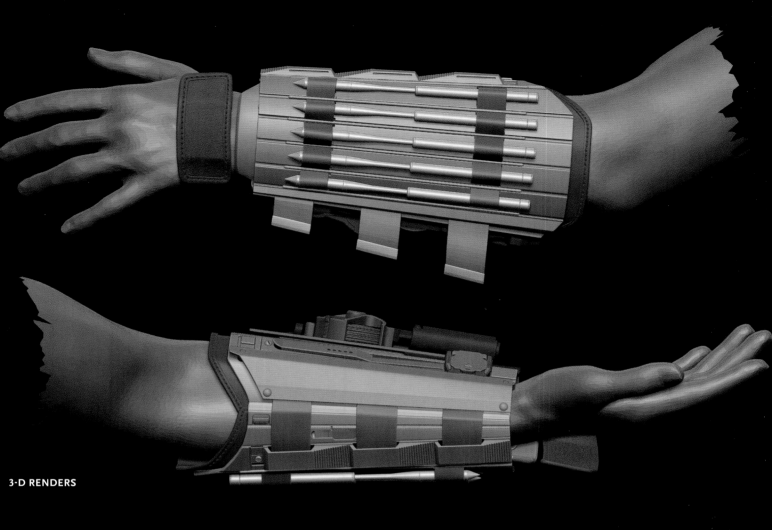

3-D RENDERS

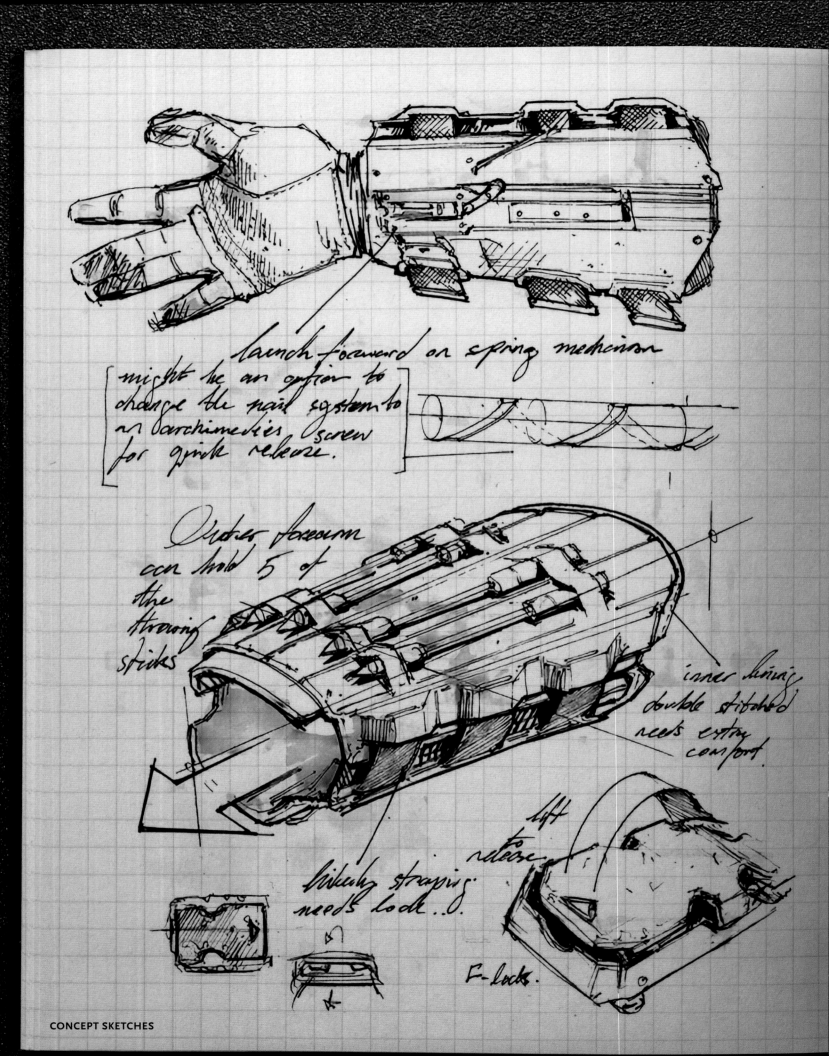

launch forward or spring mechanism

[might be an option to change the nail system to an archimedies screw for quick release.]

Outer forearm can hold 5 of the throwing sticks

inner lining double stitched needs extra comfort.

lift to release

likely strapping needs lock...

F-locks.

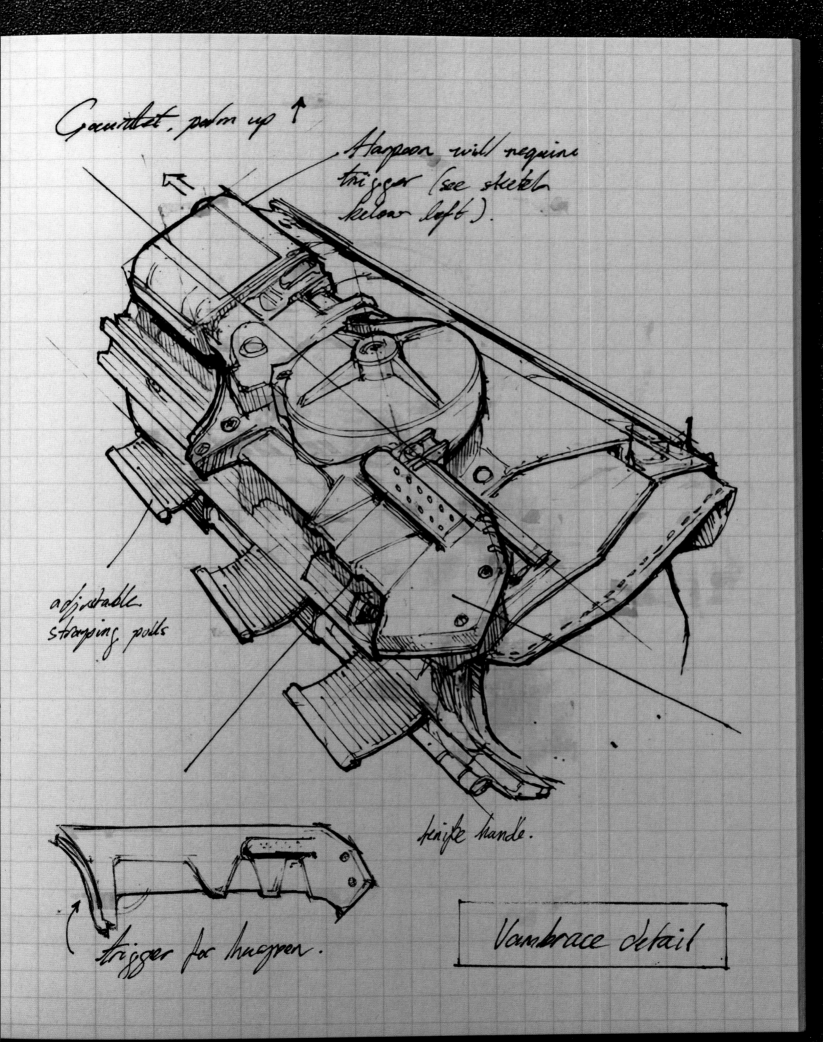

Gauntlet, palm up ↑

Harpoon will require
trigger (see sketch
below left).

adjustable
strapping pads

knife handle.

(trigger for harpoon.

Vambrace detail

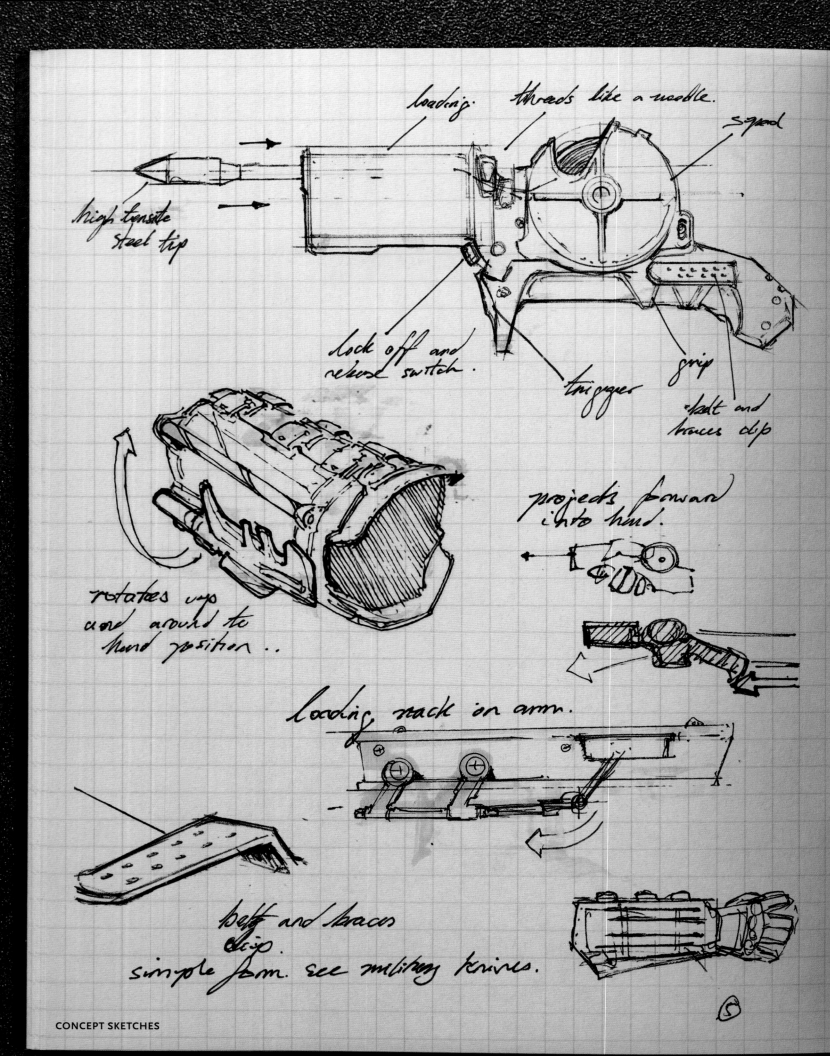

loading.

threads like a needle.

spool

high tensile
steel tip

lock off and
release switch.

trigger

grip

belt and
braces clip

rotates up
and around to
hand position ..

projects forward
into hand.

loading rack on arm.

belt and braces
clip.
simple form. see military knives.

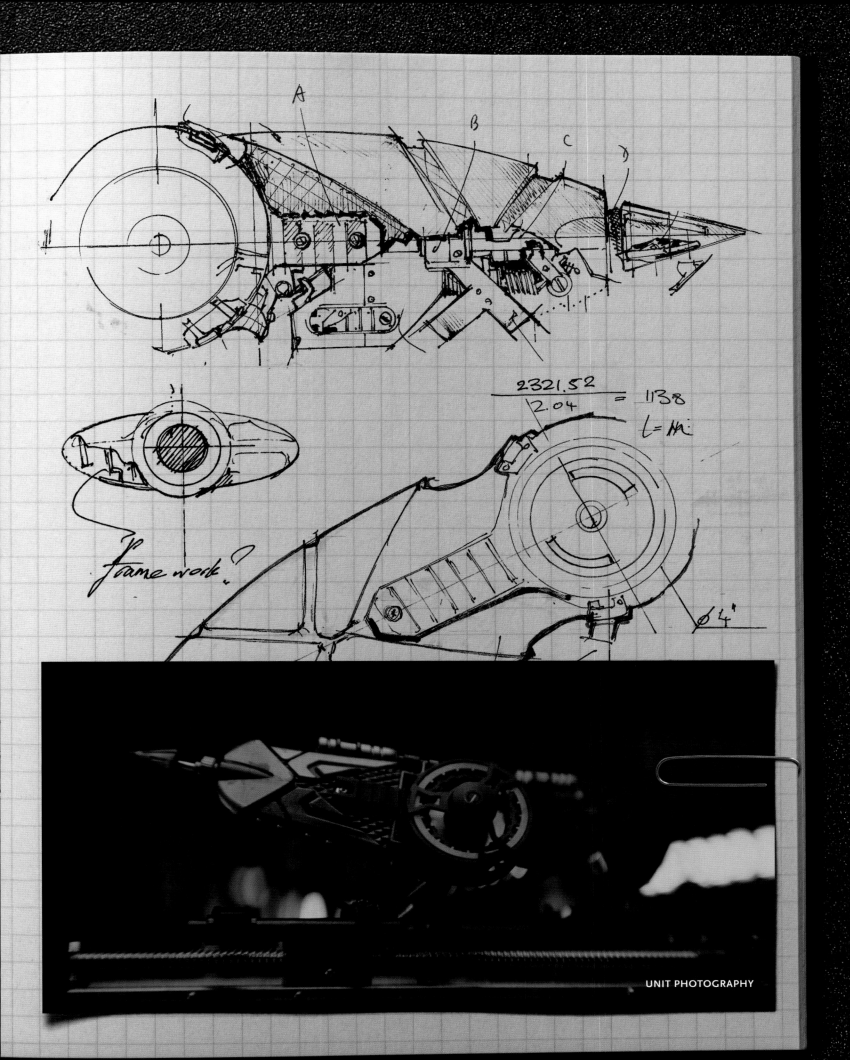

A
B
C
D

$$\frac{2321.52}{2.04} = 1138$$

$L = M$

frame work!

ϕ 4"

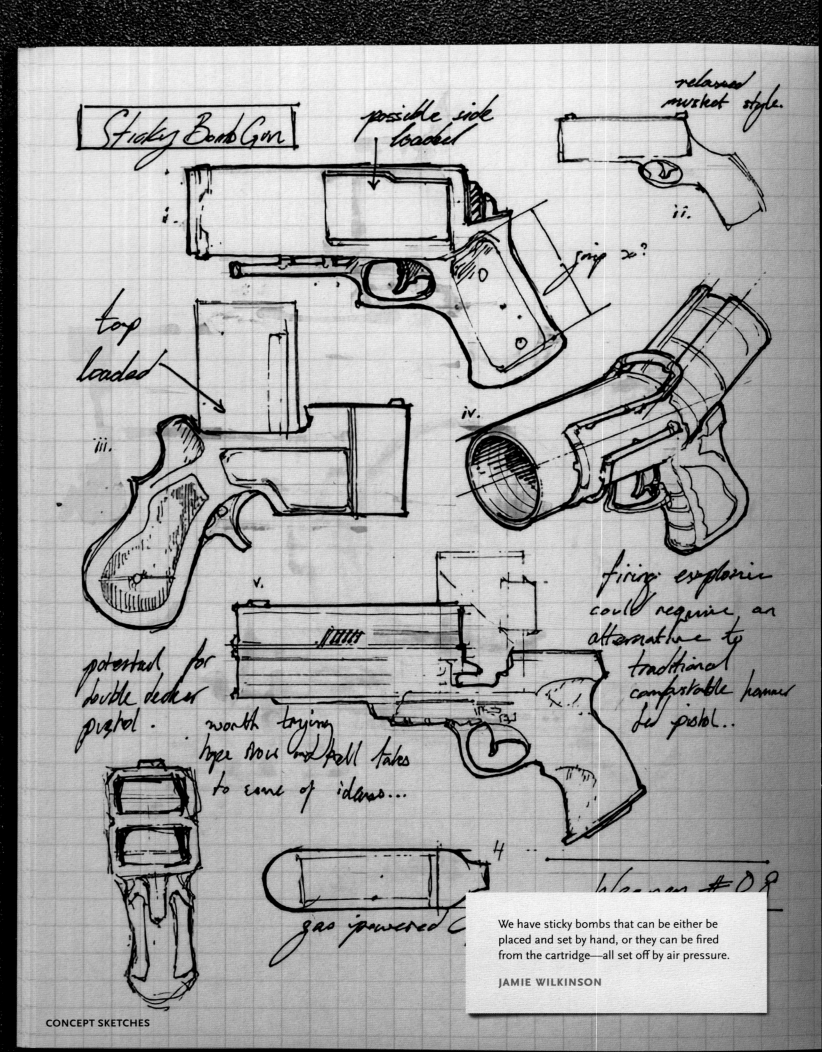

Sticky Bomb Gun

possible side loaded

released musket style.

i.

ii.

grip x?

top loaded

iii.

iv.

v.

potential for double decker pistol.. worth toying

hope Nous and Nell takes to some of ideas...

firing explosive could require an alternative to traditional comfortable hammer fed pistol..

4

gas powered C

We have sticky bombs that can be either be placed and set by hand, or they can be fired from the cartridge—all set off by air pressure.

JAMIE WILKINSON

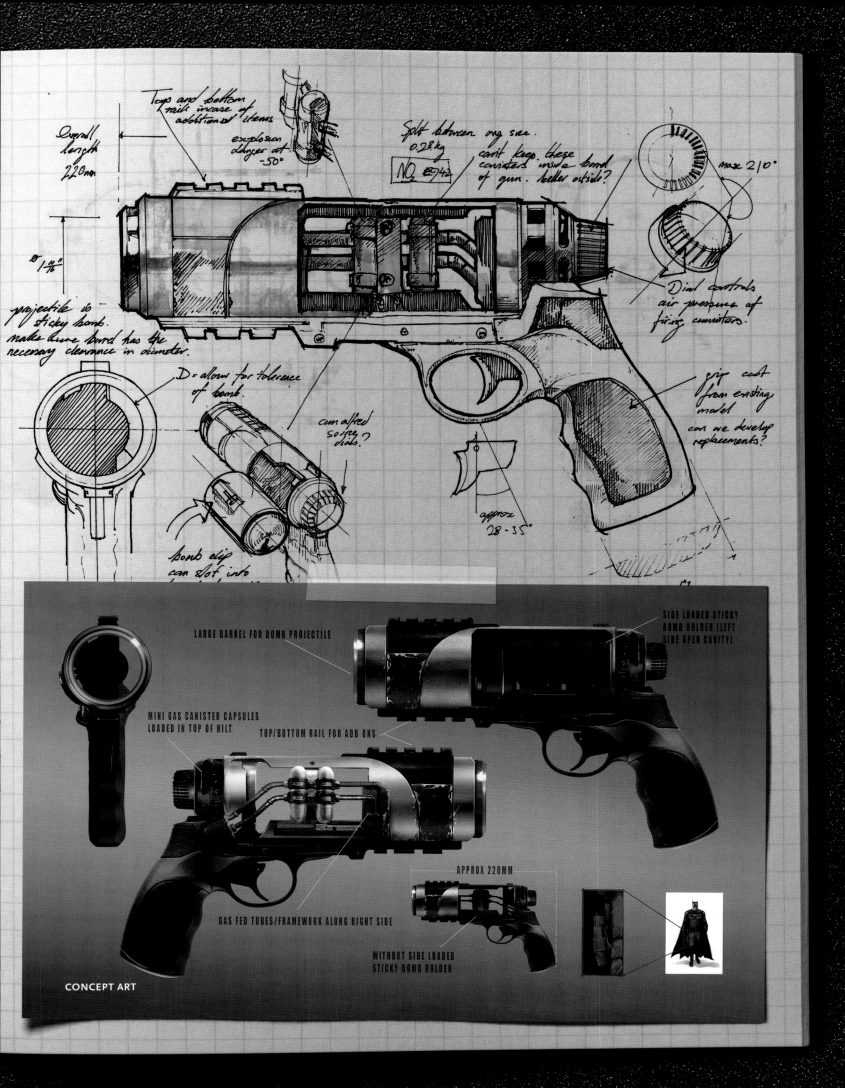

Overall length 220mm

Tops and bottom rail incase of additional items

explosion danger at ~50°

Split between mag size 0.28kg
NO_2 $E742$

can't keep these canisters inside a bomb of gun. better outside?

max 210°

Dial controls air pressure of firing canisters.

projectile is sticky bomb.
make sure barrel has the necessary clearance in diameter.

D = allow for tolerance of bomb.

can afford sources dials?

grip cast from existing model
can we develop replacements?

approx 28-35°

Bomb clip can slot into

SIDE LOADED STICKY BOMB HOLDER (LEFT SIDE OPEN CAVITY)

LARGE BARREL FOR BOMB PROJECTILE

MINI GAS CANISTER CAPSULES LOADED IN TOP OF HILT

TOP/BOTTOM RAIL FOR ADD ONS

APPROX 220MM

GAS FED TUBES/FRAMEWORK ALONG RIGHT SIDE

WITHOUT SIDE LOADED STICKY BOMB HOLDER

CONCEPT ART

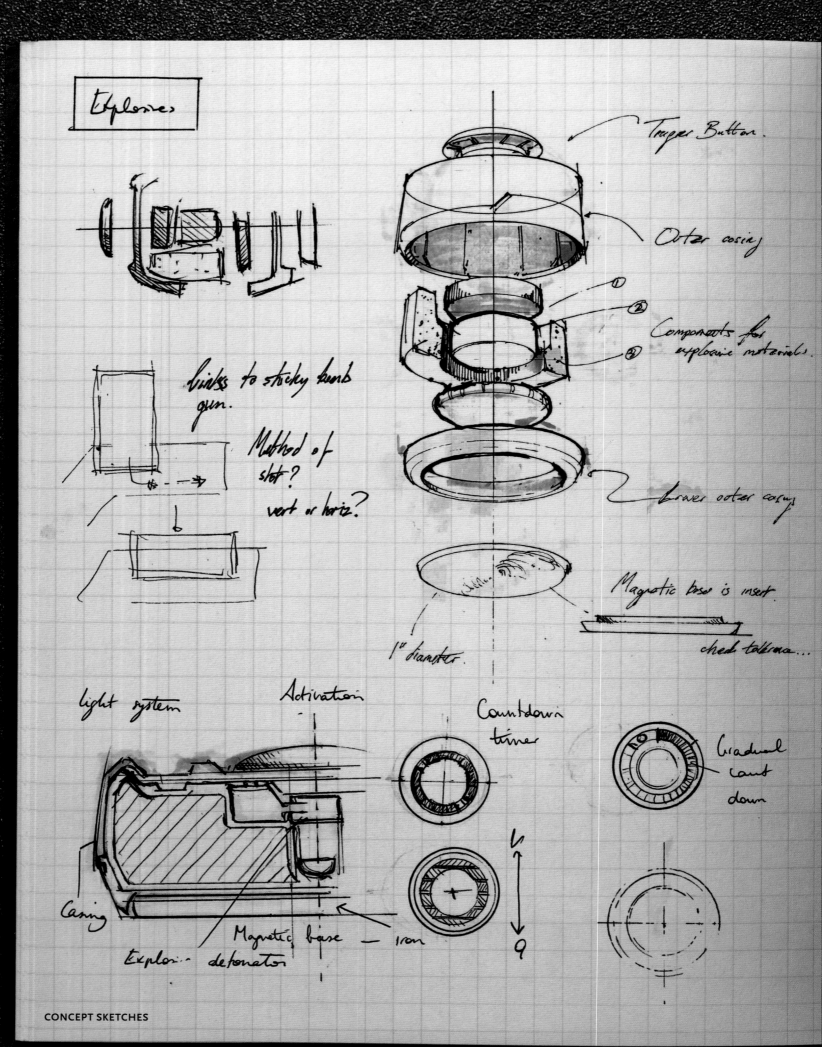

Explosives

Trigger Button.

Outer casing

Components for explosive materials.

Lower outer casing

Magnetic base is insert

1" diameter.

ched tolerna...

links to sticky bomb gun.

Method of slot?

vert or horiz?

light system

Activation

Countdown timer

Gradual count down

Casing

Magnetic base — iron

Explosi.. detonator

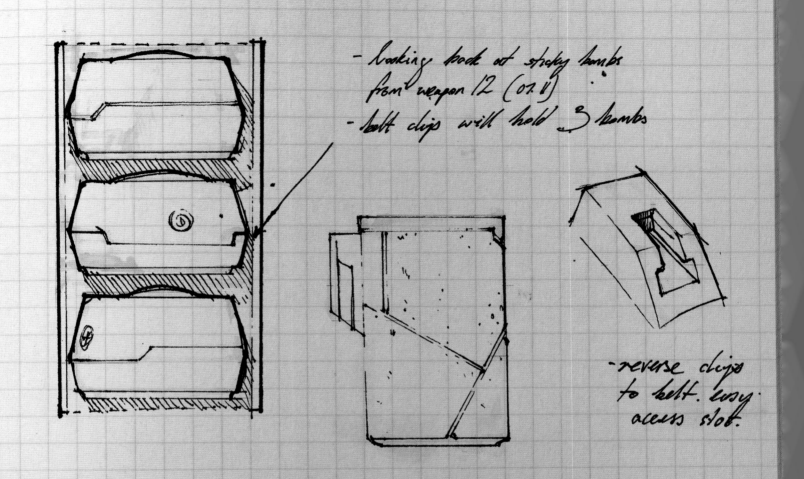

- looking back at sticky bombs from weapon 12 (or 11)
- belt clips will hold 3 bombs
- reverse clips to belt. easy access slot.

MAGNETIC BASE

THUMB ACTIVATION ON TOP

DISPENSES OUT FROM BELT

SCALE

ILLUMINATED COUNTDOWN READOUT

CONCEPT ART

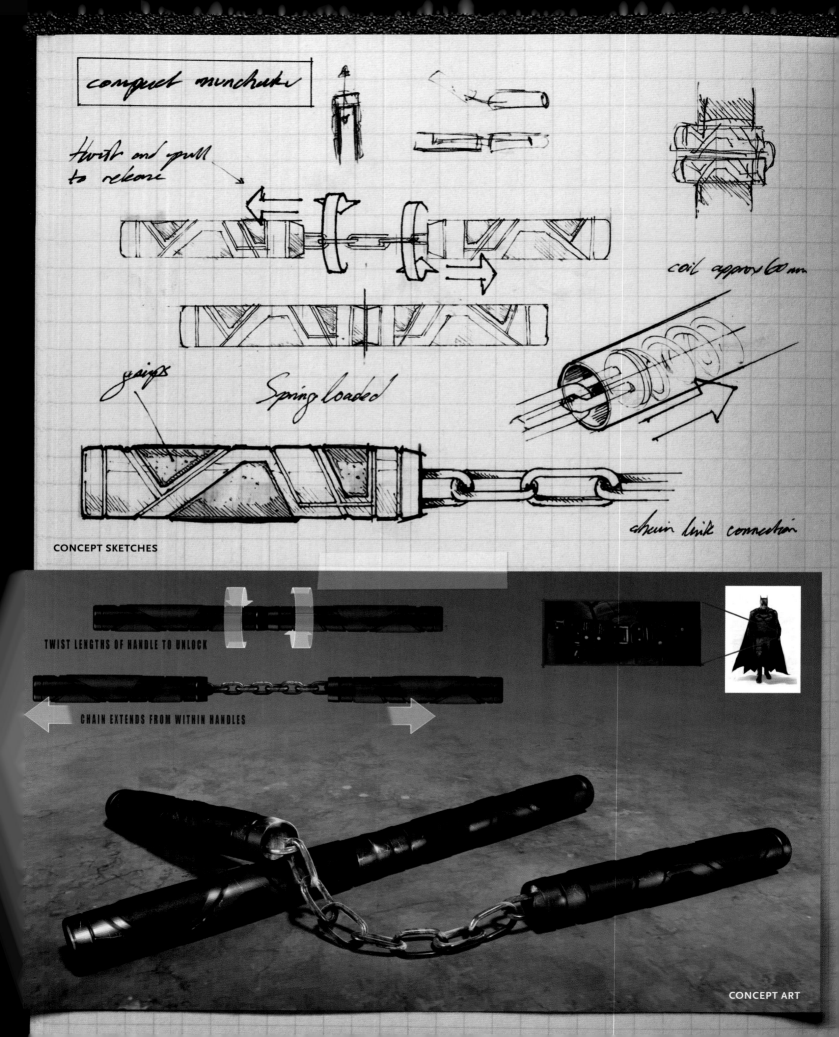

compact nunchaku

twist and pull
to release

coil approx 60mm

Spring loaded

grips

chain link connection

CONCEPT SKETCHES

TWIST LENGTHS OF HANDLE TO UNLOCK

CHAIN EXTENDS FROM WITHIN HANDLES

CONCEPT ART

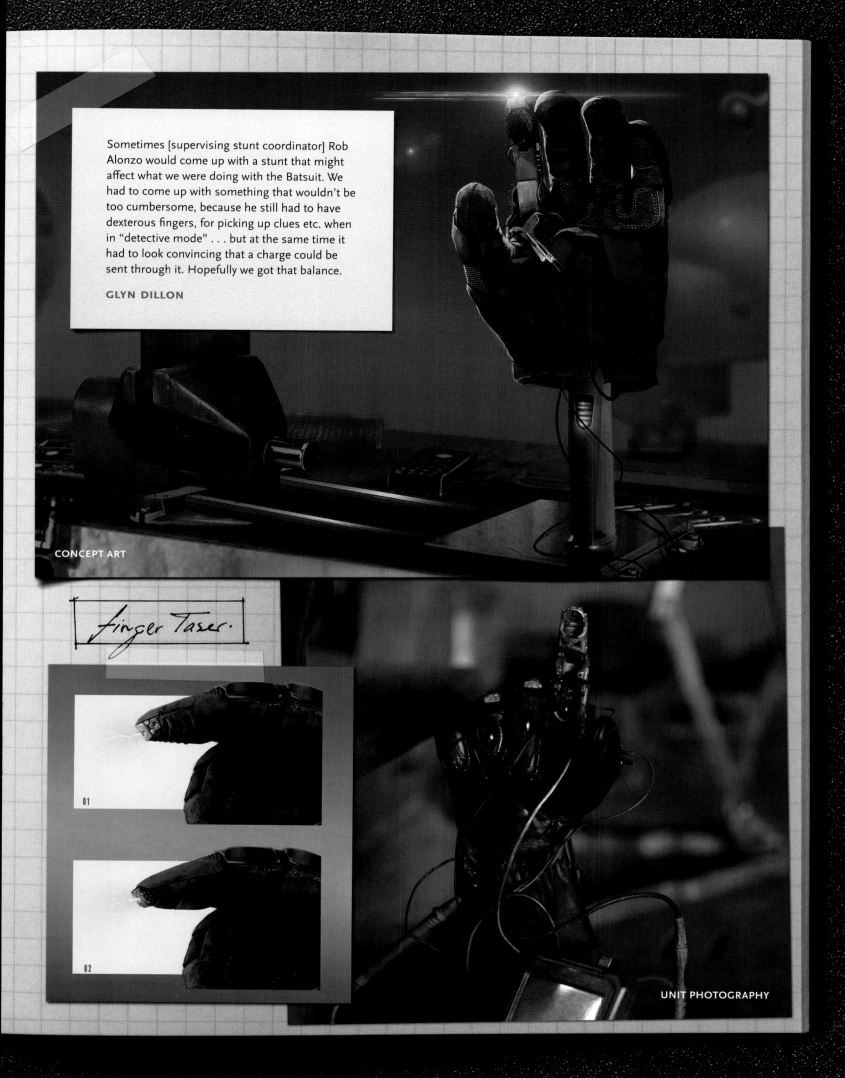

Sometimes [supervising stunt coordinator] Rob Alonzo would come up with a stunt that might affect what we were doing with the Batsuit. We had to come up with something that wouldn't be too cumbersome, because he still had to have dexterous fingers, for picking up clues etc. when in "detective mode" . . . but at the same time it had to look convincing that a charge could be sent through it. Hopefully we got that balance.

GLYN DILLON

CONCEPT ART

finger Taser.

01

02

UNIT PHOTOGRAPHY

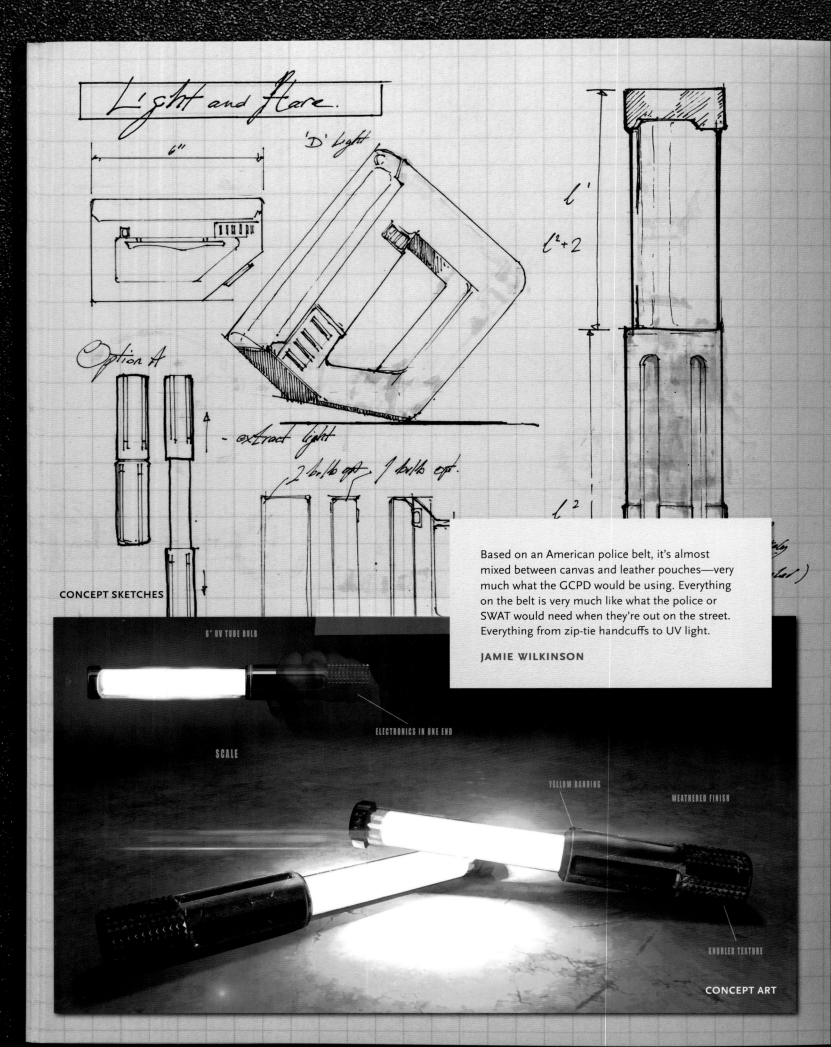

Light and flare.

6"

'D' light

l'

l² + 2

Option A

– extract light

2 bulb opt. 1 bulb opt.

l²

CONCEPT SKETCHES

6" UV TUBE BULB

ELECTRONICS IN ONE END

SCALE

Based on an American police belt, it's almost mixed between canvas and leather pouches—very much what the GCPD would be using. Everything on the belt is very much like what the police or SWAT would need when they're out on the street. Everything from zip-tie handcuffs to UV light.

JAMIE WILKINSON

YELLOW BANDING

WEATHERED FINISH

KNURLED TEXTURE

CONCEPT ART

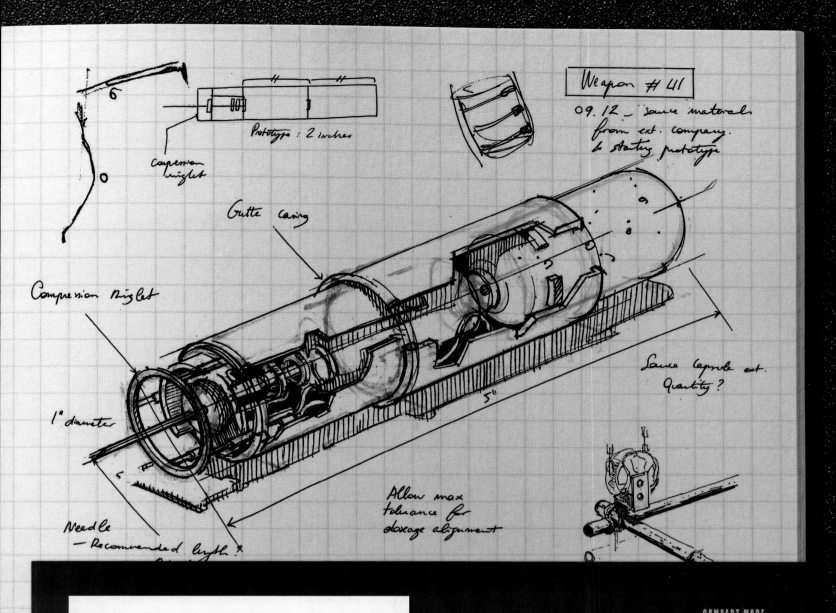

Weapon #41

09.12 — source materials from ext. company. to starting prototype

Prototype: 2 inches

Compression bridget

Gutter casing

Compression Bridget

1" diameter

Needle
— Recommended length?

Allow max tolerance for dosage alignment

Same capsule out. Quantity?

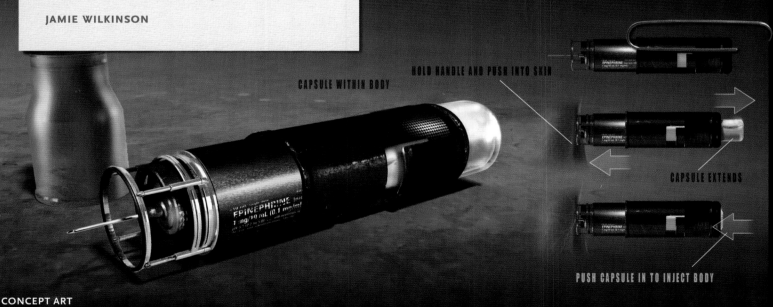

In emergencies, if he himself or somebody might need an adrenaline shot in a situation, this would be pumped in, and a shot of adrenaline straight into the system.

JAMIE WILKINSON

COMPACT MODE

REMOVE CAP

HOLD HANDLE AND PUSH INTO SKIN

CAPSULE WITHIN BODY

CAPSULE EXTENDS

PUSH CAPSULE IN TO INJECT BODY

CONCEPT ART

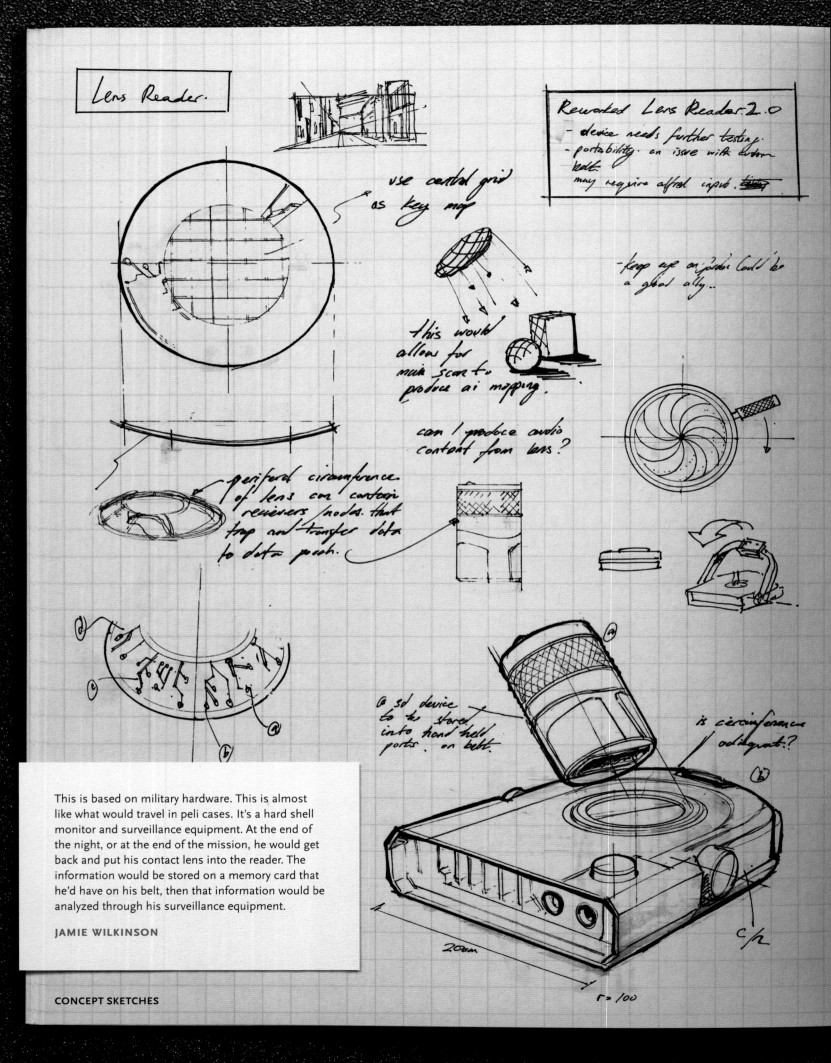

Lens Reader.

Reworked Lens Reader 2.0
- device needs further testing.
- portability. an issue with custom belt.
- may require altred input.

use central grid as key map

this would allow for mask scan to produce ai mapping.

keep eye on jordan Could be a good ally..

can I produce audio content from lens?

periferal circumference of lens can contain recievers /nodes. that trap and transfer data to data push.

a sd device to be stored into hand held ports. on belt.

is circumference/odd aspect?

This is based on military hardware. This is almost like what would travel in peli cases. It's a hard shell monitor and surveillance equipment. At the end of the night, or at the end of the mission, he would get back and put his contact lens into the reader. The information would be stored on a memory card that he'd have on his belt, then that information would be analyzed through his surveillance equipment.

JAMIE WILKINSON

20cm

c/2

r=100

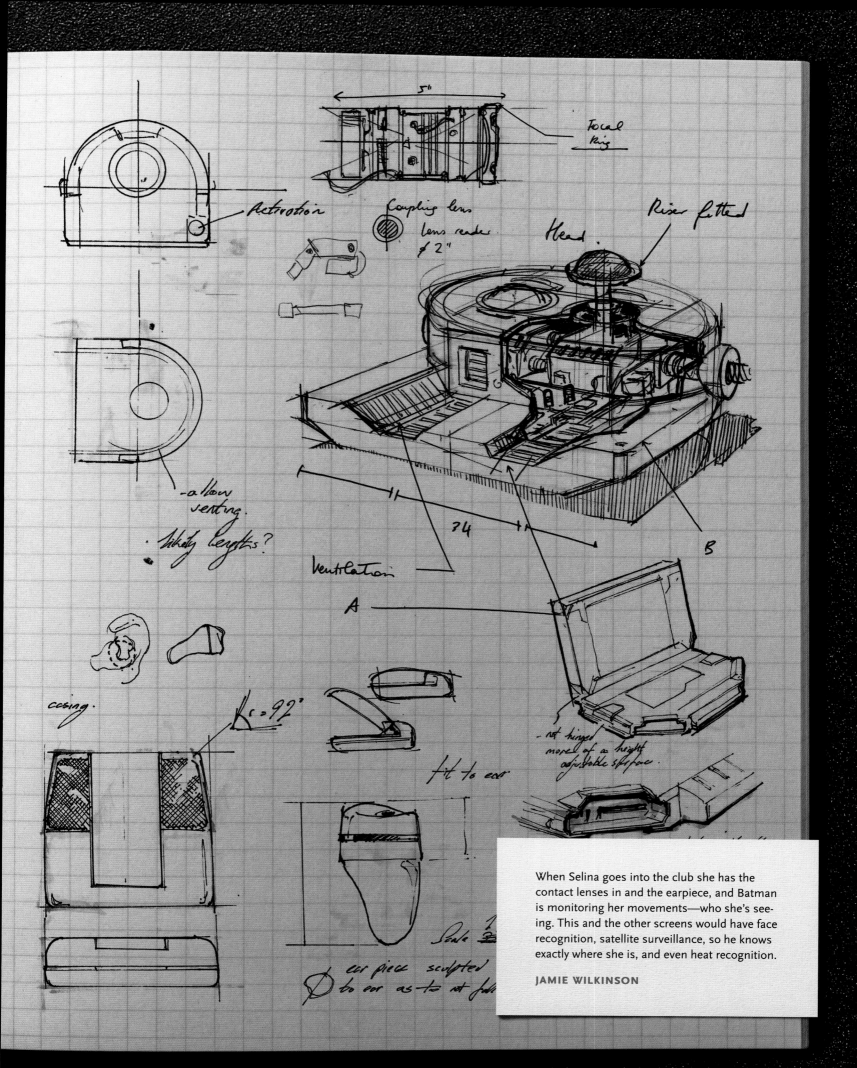

When Selina goes into the club she has the contact lenses in and the earpiece, and Batman is monitoring her movements—who she's seeing. This and the other screens would have face recognition, satellite surveillance, so he knows exactly where she is, and even heat recognition.

JAMIE WILKINSON

I wanted the purpose of The Batmobile to be very clear, which was that it was meant to terrify and intimidate—and it had to be a muscle car because it needed to perform.

MATT REEVES

THE BATMOBILE

Roaring into action for the first time in *Detective Comics #27* alongside "The Bat-Man" was another legendary staple of Batman lore, and one of the world's most iconic vehicles—The Batmobile. However, it was never properly named and, being a stately red car, it looked more like something that contemporary audiences might associate with Bruce Wayne. A few years later came a modified red convertible, dubbed "The Batmobile," while 1950 saw a version full to the brim with gadgets and gizmos that would assist with The Caped Crusader's crime fighting— a trend that would be stripped back or heightened depending on each new iteration of the car, and largely reflective of the period in time in which the car was used. "There was this amazing day when they opened up the Warner Bros. vault and we saw the Tim Burton Batmobile," recalled director Matt Reeves. "We saw all the iterations up through Zack Snyder's, and first of all, the scale of the cars is crazy; they're really, really big. But they also are a lot more fantastical—certainly the Burton ones are almost like what I'd call gothic rockets; they're just so stylized."

Striving for a more realistic take on Batman, from design through to character, a fittingly grounded Batmobile was required—a vehicle that Bruce Wayne could easibly build. Together with production designer James Chinlund they set about working out what that might look like. "When you look at the other *Batman* films, for example the Tim Burton car or the Tumbler in Chris Nolan's, each of those fit the design of those movies perfectly," began Chinlund. "I think Tim Burton's car had this super pushed aesthetic which fit into the rest of that world seamlessly. The Tumbler, which is one of my favorite Batmobiles, this amazing piece of design coming from Wayne Industries, supported the idea of Bruce as this playboy and ingrained in this military-industrial complex. Then it gets to our car, and for us and Matt, the idea was to imagine that Bruce is just so driven, he's trying to figure out 'How can I solve these problems for Gotham? How can I become this vision of vengeance?'" For director Matt Reeves, there was a requirement for The Batmobile to be emblematic of Batman. "What was important to me was that when Batman appears in the movie, he materializes out of the shadows," said Reeves. "It was important that the Batsuit, like something out of a David Lynch

movie, would grow like a terrifying apparition out of the darkness—and yet when you finally looked at it up close, you saw the seams, the stitching, a sense of how it was created. I wanted the same thing with the car, as it had exactly the same purpose. Why would you have a Batmobile? The point of The Batmobile, other than looking super cool in the movie, is to intimidate, to create terror." However, to design a car with the power to frighten required Reeves and the filmmaking team to draw upon dark and daring inspiration.

"I wanted the movie to be like a horror film in that sense," Reeves continued. "The moment of the car itself appearing for the very first time out of the shadows, in the same way that Batman does the first time we see him in his suit, that was the critical thing. There's a Stephen King story that John Carpenter made into a movie years ago called *Christine*. And I talked about how the car in that story was like a terrifying beast. Our Batmobile had to feel like a monster emerging from darkness." Reeves would work closely with director of photography Greig Fraser to identify the particular lighting that would accentuate the vehicle's striking silhouette, starting with small scale models so that they could understand how the light hits and amplifies The Batmobile's impact.

Without the engineering department of his father's company supplying the parts, this iconic vehicle had to be something Bruce could build in the bowels of Wayne Tower. "He loves American design and muscle cars, and he's a bit of a gearhead, so perhaps he took this old car that he had, cut the top off, rebuilt the frame," continued Chinlund. "I just loved the physicality of this idea that he's sort of saying 'The Charger's cool, but how can I make it my own? And I need it to be more powerful. I need it to be able to penetrate walls and blow through obstacles.'" The requirement for a Batmobile that could continually push forward, no matter what was in front of it, meant that the vehicle had a certain requirement of function over form—an impenetrable steel frame and bumper that formed the skeleton of the vehicle, as if Bruce had built everything else around it. It also needed to have masses of speed, to pursue Batman's enemies aggressively and effortlessly, and possess a stealth-like quality that would allow The World's Greatest Detective to traverse the city streets undetected. To bring the concept to life, Chinlund enlisted the expertise of award-winning special effects supervisor Dominic Tuohy (*1917*, *Star Wars: The Rise of Skywalker*, *Edge of Tomorrow*). The challenge for Tuohy and his team was to take what was in the concept art on the page and work out how to make this version of The Batmobile a reality. "Our special effects CAD [computer-aided design] engineer guys look at it, and we collectively look at what we can do in the space that we've got," said Tuohy. "Having worked on other projects where we've done similar kind of things, we then start going, 'Okay, what engine should we use for this? What transmission? Should it be four-wheel drive? Should it be two-wheel drive? Should it have a lot of suspension travel because we are gonna make this vehicle jump? How big are the wheels?' And it goes on and on and on. And it's a big jigsaw puzzle of which when you start, your problems, you see them straightway. That's the beauty of making something from scratch, that you're trying to solve those problems. And it doesn't matter how long you've been in this industry, there's always a problem that's struck up. And The Batmobile is no different."

The resulting Batmobile ended up being four different vehicles—three with gasoline engines, and one electric car that allowed for the implementation of special effects. "We're gonna introduce a lot of flame into our Batmobile, something that's not been done before," revealed Tuohy. "And by using an electric motor, that allows us the space to be able to put all of our special effects equipment into the front of it. We have used electric vehicles before—they are the future, and we're embracing it on this one." For James Chinlund, the road to developing an iconic new vehicle had been one worth travelling down. "To finally see Robert sitting in this thing, it's been such a journey. I just stand here like on the shoulders of this incredible team that put this thing together."

CONCEPT ART

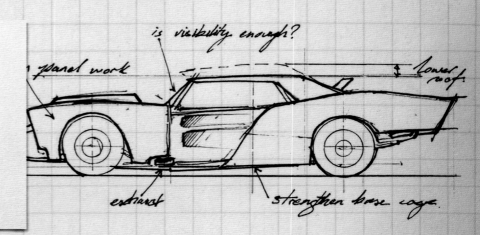

Particularly in its top shot or any sort of higher angle, you can really see the cowl motif. So, I love the way it sort of reveals itself in different angles to be more or less bat-like. The design process was like finding a way of letting Bruce reveal his character and the intimidation factor of recognizing like "Oh, my God. That's Batman!"—but at the same time keeping it under wraps and low-key.

JAMES CHINLUND

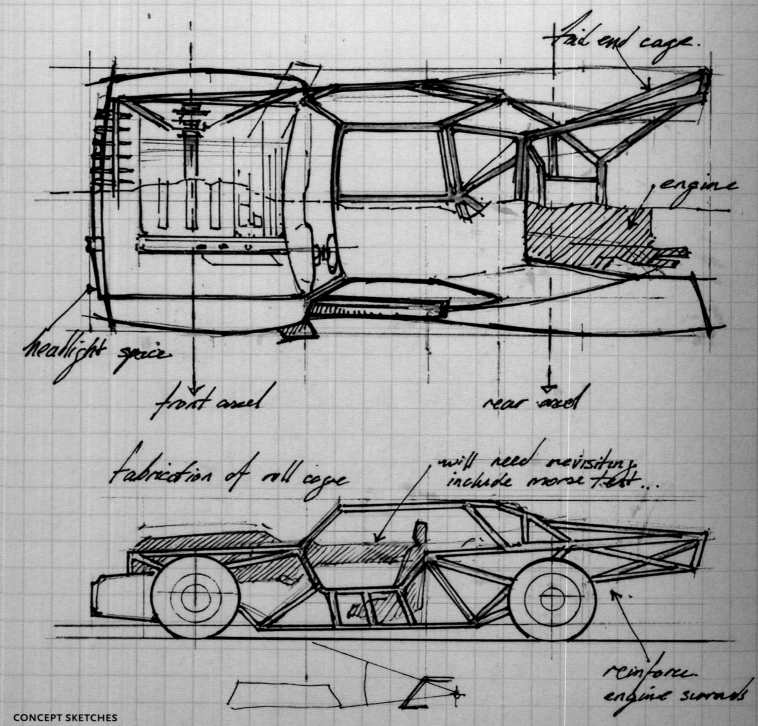

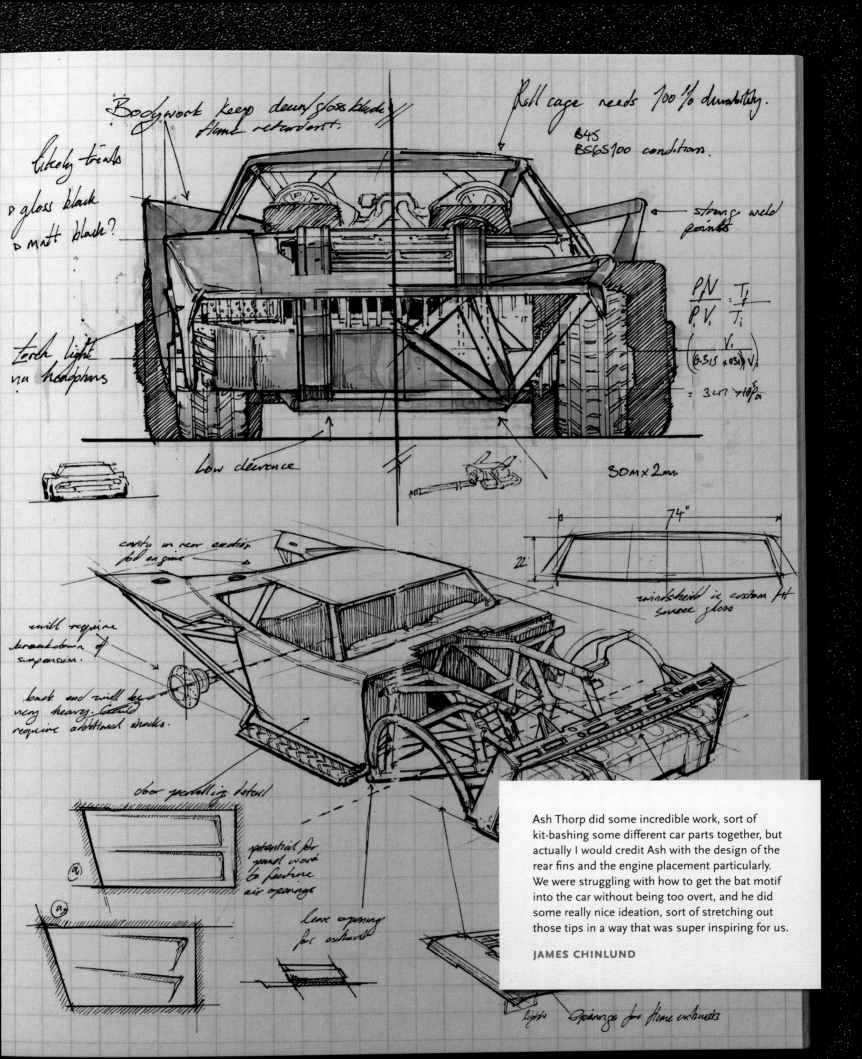

Ash Thorp did some incredible work, sort of kit-bashing some different car parts together, but actually I would credit Ash with the design of the rear fins and the engine placement particularly. We were struggling with how to get the bat motif into the car without being too overt, and he did some really nice ideation, sort of stretching out those tips in a way that was super inspiring for us.

JAMES CHINLUND

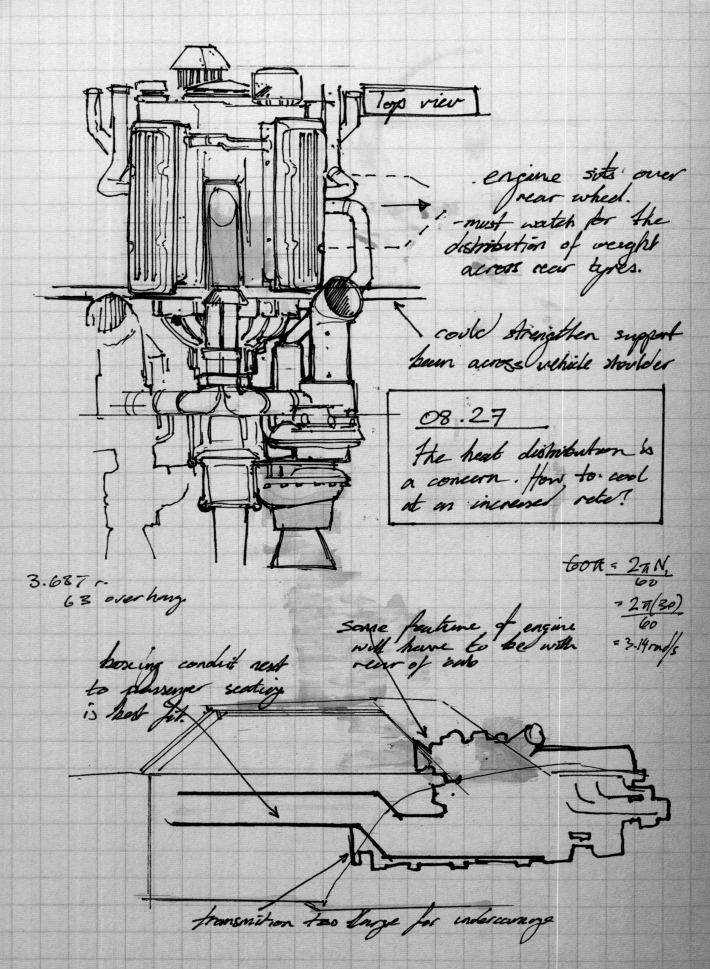

Top view

- engine sits over rear wheel.
- must watch for the distribution of weight across rear tyres.

could strengthen support beam across vehicle shoulder

08.27

The heat distribution is a concern. How to cool at an increased rate?

3.68T r.
63 overhang

boxing conduit next to passenger seating is best fit.

Some feature of engine will have to be with rear of auto

$$60\pi = \frac{2\pi N_1}{60}$$

$$= \frac{2\pi(30)}{60}$$

$$= 3.14 \, rad/s$$

transmition too large for undercarriage

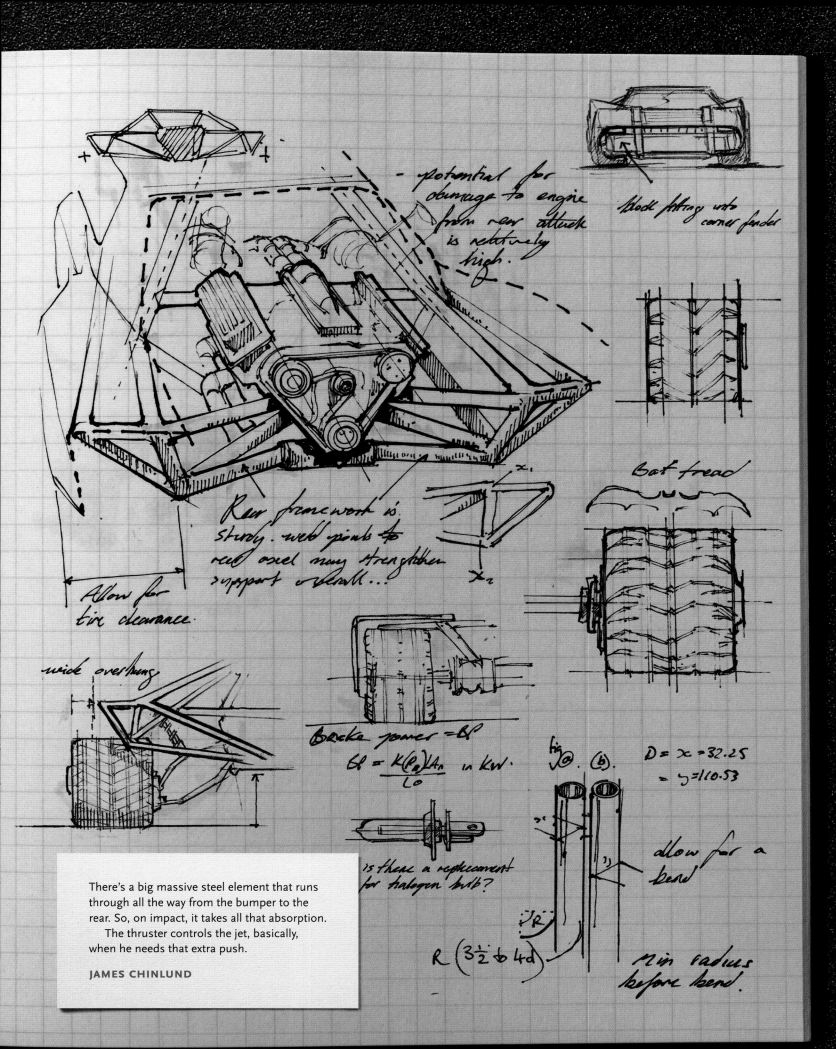

There's a big massive steel element that runs through all the way from the bumper to the rear. So, on impact, it takes all that absorption.
  The thruster controls the jet, basically, when he needs that extra push.

JAMES CHINLUND

We're specifically trying not to do anything that was overtly designed. We really wanted it to be a car that could drive through Gotham without drawing huge amounts of attention.

We wanted to make not only something that fit the story, but also something that would please the fans and be this object of desire.

JAMES CHINLUND

THE BAT BIKE

Unlike The Batmobile, the debut of The Bat Bike came much later down the line—not in the comics, but rather in the 1966 *Batman* television series (complete with a sidecar). Having been a staple of Batman's roster of vehicles ever since, The Bat Bike provides the hero with a terrifically speedy way to traverse Gotham. However, for its inclusion in *The Batman*, the bike needed to follow the same thought process as The Batmobile. "I have to say, the design process on The Bat Bike was incredibly streamlined," mused production designer James Chinlund. "We loved its simplicity and the idea that it was this kind of brutal, heavy, chunky piece of cast-metal muscle. It follows The Batmobile in that way, in that it's like a heavy, punishing, straight-ahead machine."

The electric Bat Bike was designed to feel as tangible, customized, and hand-built as The Batmobile—but its final appearance took inspiration from the Batsuit itself. "Between the cowl and the tail, I think we felt like we were playing with Batman's cowl and cape shapes," said Chinlund. "There are cowls that are very similar in racing bikes, with a few modifications. So, it was exciting for us to imagine Bruce in his workshop playing with parts."

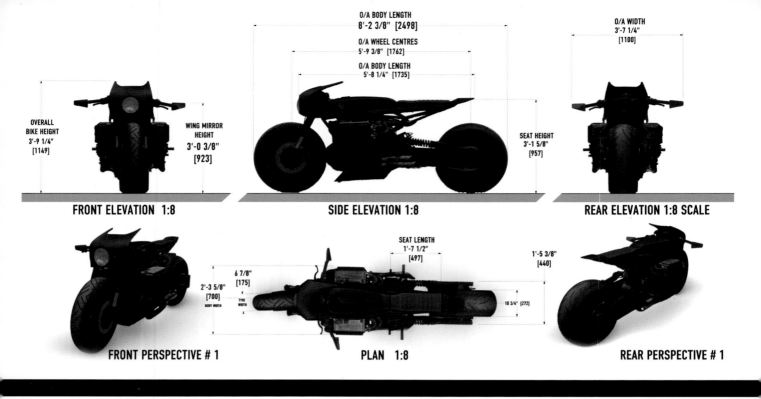

FRONT ELEVATION 1:8

OVERALL BIKE HEIGHT
3'-9 1/4" [1149]

WING MIRROR HEIGHT
3'-0 3/8" [923]

SIDE ELEVATION 1:8

O/A BODY LENGTH
8'-2 3/8" [2498]

O/A WHEEL CENTRES
5'-9 3/8" [1762]

O/A BODY LENGTH
5'-8 1/4" [1735]

SEAT HEIGHT
3'-1 5/8" [957]

REAR ELEVATION 1:8 SCALE

O/A WIDTH
3'-7 1/4" [1100]

FRONT PERSPECTIVE # 1

PLAN 1:8

6 7/8" [175]
2'-3 5/8" [700] BODY WIDTH
TYRE WIDTH

SEAT LENGTH
1'-7 1/2" [497]

1'-5 3/8" [440]
10 3/4" [272]

REAR PERSPECTIVE # 1

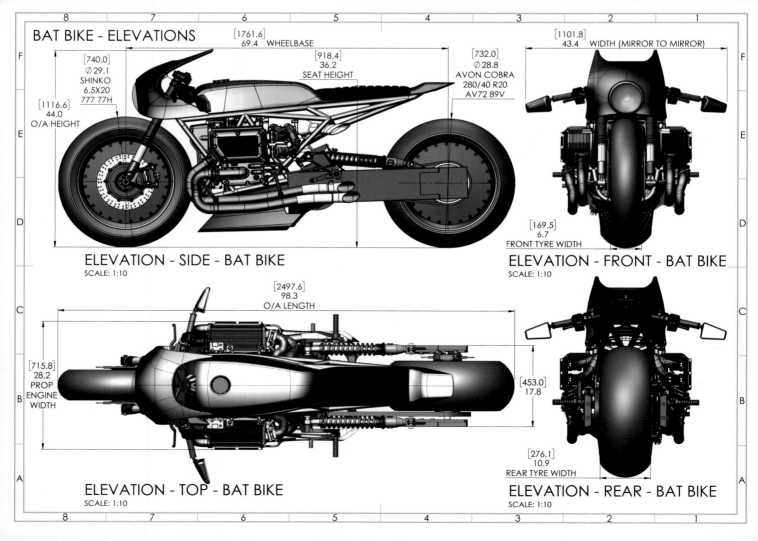

BAT BIKE - ELEVATIONS

[1761.6] 69.4 WHEELBASE

[740.0] Ø 29.1 SHINKO 6.5X20 777 77H

[918.4] 36.2 SEAT HEIGHT

[732.0] Ø 28.8 AVON COBRA 280/40 R20 AV72 89V

[1116.6] 44.0 O/A HEIGHT

ELEVATION - SIDE - BAT BIKE
SCALE: 1:10

[1101.8] 43.4 WIDTH (MIRROR TO MIRROR)

[169.5] 6.7 FRONT TYRE WIDTH

ELEVATION - FRONT - BAT BIKE
SCALE: 1:10

[2497.6] 98.3 O/A LENGTH

[715.8] 28.2 PROP ENGINE WIDTH

ELEVATION - TOP - BAT BIKE
SCALE: 1:10

[453.0] 17.8

[276.1] 10.9 REAR TYRE WIDTH

ELEVATION - REAR - BAT BIKE
SCALE: 1:10

CONCEPT ART

I was really excited about the idea of this defensive posture from the front, that we see this smooth face, and matte and dark and low profile, and then just a ton of power from the rear. And that he wasn't really focused on any protection from the back, because he's always driving forward. He's in pursuit. No one's chasing him, and so, that was sort of the mission statement—you know, this kind of relentless, hammer-like drive forward.

JAMES CHINLUND

WAYNE TOWER
& THE BATCAVE

A hands-on Bruce Wayne needs somewhere out-of-sight to build the armor, vehicles, and tactical weaponry required to complete the transformation into Batman. For the most part, the hero's secret hideout has been located underneath the Wayne family mansion, Wayne Manor. However, *The Batman* sees a very different setup with Bruce Wayne living an isolated life up in Wayne Tower. "Wayne Tower, in the movies, is usually the business hub of Wayne Enterprises," recalled Matt Reeves, "but we wanted to take this gothic tower and turn it into Bruce's home. It would be an old sky-scraper, long past its glory days like you might see at the base of Central Park or some grand old building in Chicago. A place the Rockefellers or Vanderbilts could have lived in." Production designer James Chinlund saw a clear connection between the choice of Wayne Tower and this incarnation of Bruce Wayne. "I'm a huge fan of a tower and not a manor. I've always found that the manor was a little dissident to me. I mean, it was like, 'Wait, so Bruce lives in the suburbs in this, like, fancy manor?'" Situated in the heart of the city, the striking structure provides a window to Gotham's more opulent past and a wealth that no longer flows

so cleanly through its streets. On the inside, the tower functions almost as a museum to Thomas and Martha Wayne—largely unchanged since the night of their murder. "For me, one of the main references for the tower was the Maysles brothers' documentary *Grey Gardens*, about a reclusive mother and daughter living alone in an old derelict New York mansion," said Matt Reeves. "The idea of getting the decay to show through so that you can see what once was but is no longer—and that sense of the beauty of decay, and how that was reflective of Bruce, of his character was key. He doesn't care about any of the traditional family history anymore. He's so into his obsessive mission, it's like a drug for him—he's addicted to being Batman. So when you look closely at the inside of Wayne Manor, it looks like somebody has just let everything fall apart."

Rather than the typical bat-filled cave, the filmmakers decided to give *The Batman* a Batcave that best fit the overall logical, reasoned approach to the story. "If the Wayne [family] built this tower in the twenties, what would be below this tower that would offer an opportunity for a cave?" asked Chinlund. "There's an underground train station at the Waldorf Astoria in New York. The myth is that there's a train parked there all the time, and the idea is that whenever the president is in town, if there's ever an emergency and he has to get out of town, they could take him through this secret tunnel at the Waldorf and get him out of town discreetly. I always loved that idea and thought it was so romantic, so I thought about the idea that if you were the Waynes and you had created this city, you would probably have your own secret train terminal under the tower."

VFX 3-D RENDER

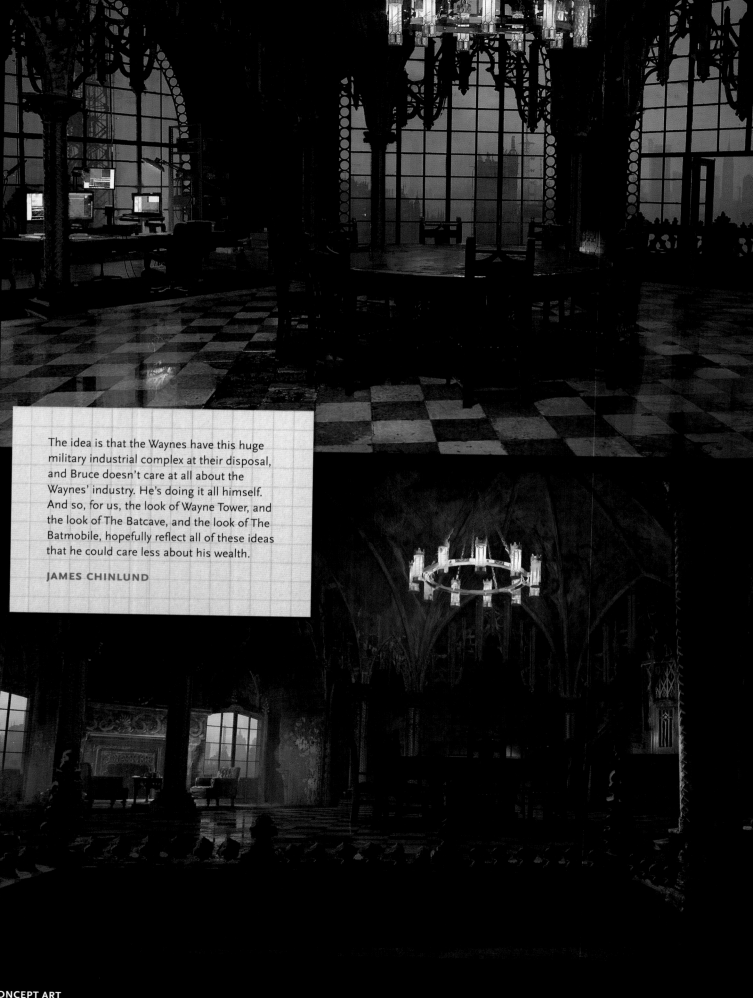

The idea is that the Waynes have this huge military industrial complex at their disposal, and Bruce doesn't care at all about the Waynes' industry. He's doing it all himself. And so, for us, the look of Wayne Tower, and the look of The Batcave, and the look of The Batmobile, hopefully reflect all of these ideas that he could care less about his wealth.

JAMES CHINLUND

CONCEPT ART

CONCEPT ART

FILM STILL

CONCEPT ART

CONCEPT ART

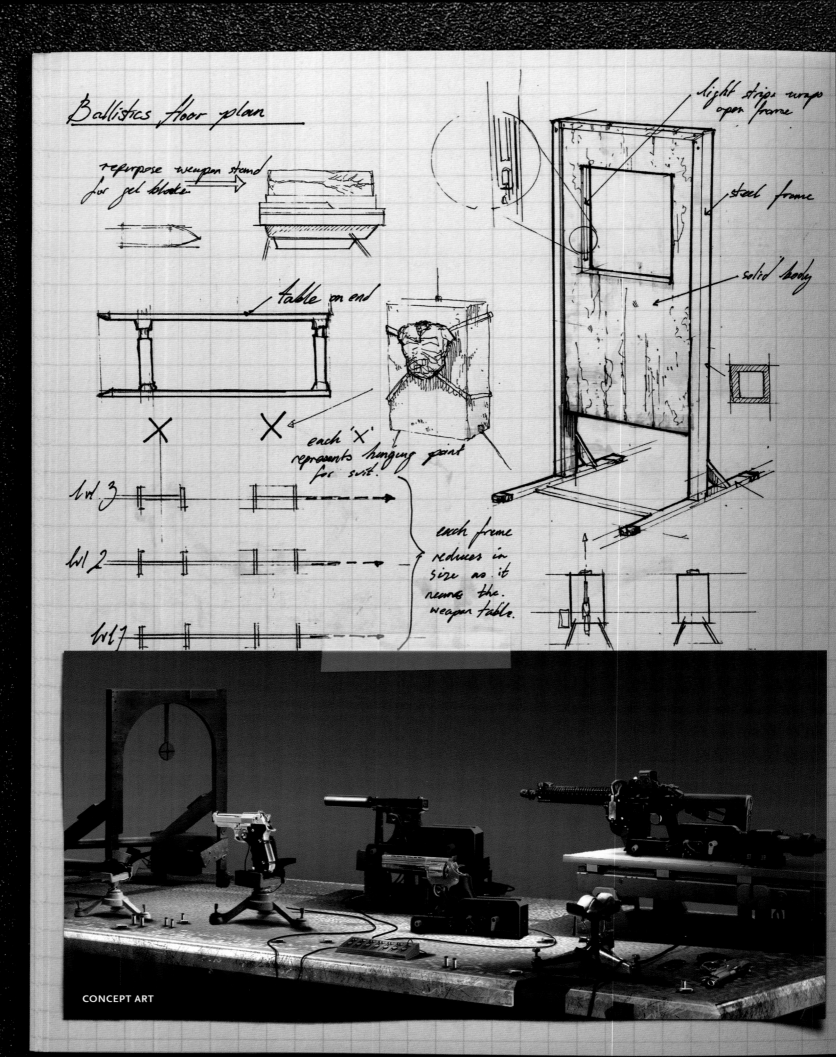

Ballistics floor plan

repurpose weapon stand for gel blade.

light strips wraps open frame

steel frame

table on end

solid body

each 'X' represents hanging point for suit.

lvl 3

lvl 2

lvl 1

each frame reduces in size as it nears the weapon table.

CONCEPT ART

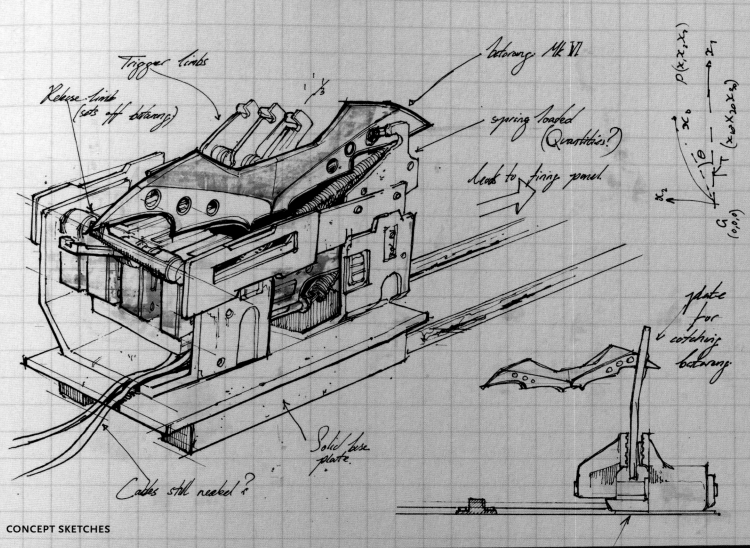

Trigger limbs

Release limb
(sets off batarang)

batarang: Mk VI

spring loaded
(Quantities?)

leads to firing panel.

plate
for
catching
batarang.

Solid base
plate.

Cables still needed?

$p(x_1,x_2,x_3)$

x_3

x_0

θ

x_1

$(x_{10}x_{20}x_{30})$

x_2

G
$(0,0,0)$

CONCEPT SKETCHES

CONCEPT ART

CONCEPT ART

UNIT PHOTOGRAPHY

BRUCE WAYNE

Originally introduced as Commissioner James Gordon's "young socialite friend" in 1939's *Case of the Chemical Syndicate*, the mustard-suited, pipe-smoking Bruce Wayne met the prospect of a visiting a crime scene with the same type of leisurely ambivalence ("Oh well, nothing else to do, might as well") that seems to have stuck with our preconceptions of Batman's extraverted billionaire alter ego. In *The Batman* we meet a Bruce Wayne who possesses a very different demeanor. "We'd already seen Bruce as the ultra-rich playboy," remarked *The Batman* director Matt Reeves. "But I wanted him to feel almost like a fallen American prince. I wanted him to be someone whose parents had been larger than life; philanthropic figures who everyone revered as Gotham royalty. And in the wake of their tragic deaths, instead of fostering the image of the storied Waynes, he completely withdrew, and became what I saw as an almost rockstar-like recluse. I saw him kind of like Kurt Cobain. There was actually a moment when I was writing when I started listening to Nirvana's "Something in the Way," and there was just something very resonant in it for me. . . . I could see Bruce like a pale, somewhat vampiric rockstar in this old, grungy manor." Inspiration for this Reeves' depiction of Bruce Wayne also came from the Gus Van Sant film *Last Days*, centred around a fictionalized Cobain-like character. "He's in this decaying old wreck

of a home, and in the living room, he's got his amps and his electric guitars, and I thought 'Well, this is our version of Bruce Wayne.'"

While Robert Pattinson's Bruce Wayne still drives an impeccably cool car (a split-window 1963 Chevrolet Corvette Sting Ray), and possesses a minimalistic yet expensive wardrobe, every single stylistic choice was made to reflect a significant internal struggle. Academy Award–winning costume designer Jacqueline Durran (*Little Women* [2019], *1917*, *Anna Karenina* [2012]) recalled working with the lead actor to establish the character's appearance. "He had loads of thoughts, Robert. It was all about honing it down and making it less. It was always about taking away rather than adding. How do you represent someone of his wealth and stature, and at the same time represent his psychological situation? So that was the balancing act really. He doesn't look like a playboy. He's more like a tortured soul." However, the transformation from a pained, brooding Master Wayne into the terrifying Batman required more than just a cape and cowl. Actor Jeffrey Wright, taking on the role of the hero's trusted ally and Gotham City Police Department (GCPD) lieutenant Jim Gordon, noted a remarkable physical transformation in Pattinson's performance. "It's as though he had grown like five inches. He just had a presence about him that's not at all the way he carries himself when the camera is off. It was really beautiful just to see the transformation, the various steps of transformation that he takes in this. One is Bruce Wayne, and then the transformation that Bruce Wayne takes as Batman. It's just beautifully distinct in a way that's going to be really compelling and exciting and new."

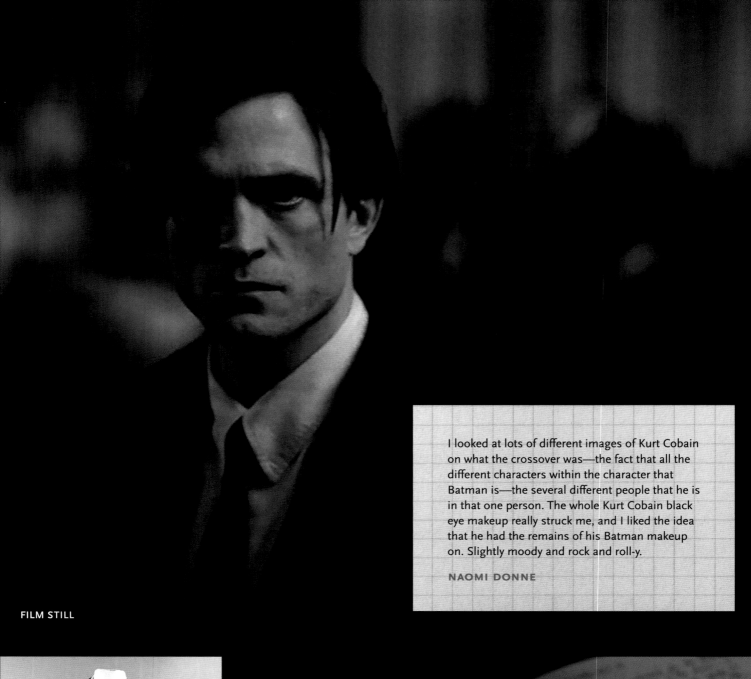

I looked at lots of different images of Kurt Cobain on what the crossover was—the fact that all the different characters within the character that Batman is—the several different people that he is in that one person. The whole Kurt Cobain black eye makeup really struck me, and I liked the idea that he had the remains of his Batman makeup on. Slightly moody and rock and roll-y.

NAOMI DONNE

FILM STILL

UNIT PHOTOGRAPHY

UNIT PHOTOGRAPHY

THE DRIFTER

With the persona of brutal, wraith-like vigilante Batman on one end of the spectrum, and the reclusive scion Bruce Wayne on the other, there was a requirement to find some semblance of a middle ground, where the character could seamlessly blend into the crowded streets of Gotham without being recognized either way. "He can't walk around in public places wearing the Batsuit, people would be like 'Who's that guy in the costume?'" said Matt Reeves. "So that's how I actually borrowed a concept that I saw in Frank Miller's *Year One*, where before he ever even adopted the suit Bruce went around sort of as an alter-ego: the drifter." It's a state that producer Dylan Clark describes as "coming out of the Batman fever dream—he's not Bruce Wayne either." In *The Batman*, the hero adopts a "drifter" costume—allowing this grounded, practical Batman to prowl the city's most dangerous locations without unwanted attention, make detailed observations on the city's comings and goings in a journal, while also carrying his Batsuit around in a backpack. "Then he transforms into Batman and . . . he confronts it. I always liked the idea,

kind of the grimy version of Superman going into the phone box," said Robert Pattinson.

"There were two influences on the Drifter costume. One was *Year One*, and one was just the idea of how you are invisible in a modern crowd. So, what do you wear?" asked costume designer Jacqueline Durran. Once again, Pattinson was hands-on with the development of this very particular look. "Rob was involved in the evolution of this costume," began Durran. "He really wanted to push the workwear, and the idea that what makes you most invisible in a modern crowd is if you're wearing some sort of uniform. He specifically spoke about the dock workers in Manhattan and the kind of workwear they wear, and you just pass in the crowd unnoticed." In addition to the costume itself, the Drifter required a bike (and accompanying bike helmet) that could maintain the level of citywide invisibility needed. The custom-built Drifter Bike combined Bruce Wayne's functional nature with that of a real-world gearhead. "We love the idea of building Bruce up as someone who has turned his back on his family's wealth and has really thrown himself into building himself from the ground up, and building all the tools, and weapons, and vehicles that he needs to execute his mission," said production designer James Chinlund. "And so, for me, the Drifter Bike really encapsulates that—you can see his aesthetic wrapped up in a nutshell. Everything you see on the bike has a function."

BATMAN: YEAR ONE   David Mazzucchelli (pencils & inks)

It was quite driven by the *Year One* comic book—this sort of hooded figure that lurks around, and we've been guided a lot by that. You never really quite see who he is, really.

We talked with Jacqueline and she was saying a lot of the drifter look was based off of this workman, blue-collar kind of look, and you can see it in the makeup too. It's not a flattering leading man makeup at all. It's quite real in a sense. It's all based in a reality that surrounds his life. It's sad.

NAOMI DONNE

Bruce's Café Racer is his undercover bike that he uses to get around town. It's built on a Honda CB750 body, and for me, this really is the beating heart of Bruce's design aesthetic, which says function first. He wants a motorcycle that he can get at and easily fix and repair, but it also has a stripped-down, lean aesthetic that I think carries forward into The Batmobile and The Bat Bike.

JAMES CHINLUND

We were interested in taking the lines and feeling of the Café Racer for Bruce, and we used a lot of that to inform the development and design in The Batmobile, in addition to The Bat Bike.

JAMES CHINLUND

Andy Serkis is delightful. From our first meeting, he just wanted Alfred to be very well-dressed. Very tailored, very neat, to have a military precision about what he wore, and that's what we tried to do. We bought vintage mohair to give the suit a sixties feel. We loved this show label on the waistcoat. That was an important detail for Andy. The collar has the kind of tab underneath that keeps it really neat. The curve is a retro curve.

It's a very traditional British Savile Row look. It almost feels like a uniform, but not quite. It's too stylish, too sartorial to actually be a uniform. Andy was just great at contributing to that. He's very proper, Alfred.

JACQUELINE DURRAN

RELATED CHARACTER
ALFRED

Having adorned the pages of Batman comics since his first appearance as Alfred Beagle in *Batman* #16 (1943), Alfred Pennyworth is the surrogate father figure and mentor to Batman—a role thrust upon him after the shocking murder of his employers, Thomas and Martha Wayne, left their ten-year-old son Bruce orphaned. "There have been so many great interpretations of Alfred, as there have been of Batman," began Andy Serkis (*The Lord of the Rings* trilogy, *Sex & Drugs & Rock & Roll*, *Black Panther*), who would become the latest actor to take on the role. "What we really talked about was the kind of untold emotional connection that is between them. Alfred has this sort of sense of survivor guilt, having been the bodyguard that let down Thomas Wayne and Martha. He feels deeply responsible." Following in the footsteps of Alan Napier, Michael Gough, Michael Caine, and Jeremy Irons, Andy Serkis brings a fascinating new take on the loyal butler. Having previously collaborated with director Matt Reeves and producer Dylan Clark on both *Dawn of the Planet of the Apes* and *War for the Planet of the Apes*, Serkis was no stranger to adding new layers of emotional depth to familiar characters and stories. "Andy has perfect access to truthful emotion, and can really make you feel something," recounted Clark. "He's also very masculine, so has this nice balance of masculinity and intimacy. Andy is just great at accessing this idea of a man just horribly pained and terrified that he's somewhat culpable for the creation of this Batman."

The relationship between Alfred and Bruce Wayne in *The Batman* goes beyond the often depicted butler-master dynamic. "There's a lot of unsaid kind of tension between Alfred and Bruce, because Alfred feels so responsible—but Alfred is not built that way," said Serkis. "He's just not able to connect in an emotional way. All of these years, there's brooding tension that's growing between them. The only thing that he could do, really, to alleviate that was to teach him how to fight. To teach him things he learned in the army, the skills, the ways of decoding messages and sort of practical things that he learnt. Alfred is just not built to be an emotional being for him, a father figure." Building upon the typical characterization of a steady sort with a stiff upper lip, the Alfred of *The Batman* has all the hallmarks of a man military-trained—precise, steeled, and stoic. Perhaps starting his career in MI5 (the UK's Security Service) or MI6 (The Secret Intelligence Service), Serkis suggested that "from then, he would have taken a job as a personal bodyguard to royals, to high-ranking politicians, and then has ended up in the Wayne household. There's an almost Victorian kind of sensibility about him in that respect in defending the honor of your employer, and you almost become part of the family, but not quite." The tension of having Bruce Wayne's most trusted adviser also be his employee is one thing, but having two emotionally affected characters trying to overcome the secrets of their shared past posed a new challenge. "Bruce really has, over the preceding few years leading up to becoming Batman and going into that, he's begun to cut him off and to become very isolated; not really responding to any sort of offers Alfred makes toward him to coax him out of that," said Serkis. "Bruce is now, as an adult, trying to find his own moral compass, his own version of what truth is, and the film very much deals with the notion of truth and lies and his navigation of that."

We wanted to ground the concept in reality and in what would be possible for these characters. So, Paul Dano and Matt were both adamant that they wanted to research what The Riddler could have found in a surplus store near his house—and that would have been the kind of perimeters of the options available to him. So, we really looked into surplus, and I think one of the defining things was finding the winter combat mask. We found it on eBay; it could have been from any kind of surplus store, and I think that gave us a way into the character. Other than that, we were just finding different elements—the German jacket, American trousers, American boots, that would just be putting them together to make those intimidating as he could.

JACQUELINE DURRAN

JUSTICE
THE RIDDLER

f Batman is the embodiment of vengeance, then what does that make the antagonist of *The Batman*, Edward Nashton, aka The Riddler? "Justice," suggested Paul Dano, the actor who would be cast as the legendary DC Super-Villain in *The Batman*. "I think a lot of it is about what's unfair, what feels fair and what's been unfair," he continued. "It's not fair that the corrupt are getting richer while we're suffering, you know? And it's justice . . . vengeance and justice, I think."

The Riddler first appeared in *Detective Comics* #140 (1948), sporting a lime green one-piece that was embellished all over with question marks. In the caper, the 'Prince of Puzzles" sends Batman on a mystery-solving trail, the first of many instances where the then-named Edward Nigma would try to outsmart and outmatch The World's Greatest Detective. Bringing such a legendary and often gregariously portrayed personality into a realistic, contemporary Batman story required a great deal of care—ensuring that the choice of villain would enhance Batman's narrative, rather than detract from it. As the film would not be an origin story, Matt Reeves saw the choice of The Riddler as an opportunity to bring Bruce Wayne's history to the forefront without directly retelling (or showing) any of the usual transformative events that would lead him to becoming Batman. "I wanted it to be a noir, like *Chinatown*—in which the city itself is a major character, and the history of Gotham's corruption is critical to understanding the whole story," revealed Reeves. As The Riddler's crimes evolve, you start to realize that there's something that the killer is trying to reveal about Gotham's true history, and that eventually leads Batman/Bruce from the case that he's trying to solve, crime by crime, to something unexpectedly personal. The Riddler's ciphers and clues start to refer unsettlingly to the Waynes' secret family history, and even to the potential reasons behind Bruce's parents' shocking murder, but without us seeing any of these things. It's all part of the city's crooked past, and an indictment from the killer about why Gotham is still so irredeemably corrupt today."

While Batman's Rogues Gallery is notoriously rich, often celebrated for the villains' deeply psychological, sympathetic backstories, The Riddler not only provided the perfect chance for Matt Reeves to create a narrative that would put the spotlight on Batman's sleuthing, but also gave way to interesting counterpoints to the hero's characterization. "Matt was very interested in setting up a parallel between The Riddler and The Batman, and so they are sort of mirrors of each other," offered production designer James Chinlund. "Both equally obsessed with rooting out the evils of Gotham, obviously working at it from different angles, but both very meticulous and detail-oriented."

If *The Batman* is Year Two for Bruce Wayne's Batman experiment, we find disillusioned young Edward Nashton in his first year of operation. "He's working as a forensic accountant and should probably be doing something a bit more meaningful or important than he is," said Paul Dano. "You have a kid named Bruce Wayne who loses his parents and responds to his trauma in his way, not with ease, but ends up trying to do something good with that pain. Then you have the trauma of somebody who's lost his parents in a different way and who takes that pain and probably thinks he's doing something good, but it is maybe misguided or misdirected—and I thought that felt like a really good way into, quote, 'a villain.'" Known for his ability to deliver both electric, intense performances in films such as *There Will Be Blood* and *Prisoners*, and sensitive, understated portrayals in the likes of *Little Miss Sunshine* and *Where the Wild Things Are*, Dano brought a human, empathetic quality to the otherwise terrifying Nashton. "Paul is very specific about his character development, and it was so exciting for us seeing him bringing The Riddler to life," said James Chinlund. "We had many deep, exciting, and interesting conversations about how we should be reflecting his world. Paul really wanted to make sure that the humanity of the character came through and that we weren't delivering some psycho off the stereotypical sort of template— we wanted to make sure the depth was there."

THE RIDDLER PERSONA

"I think he is somebody who was probably drowning in himself, in his mind, in his past, and in this city that didn't offer him a helping hand his entire life," mused Paul Dano, "and when he discovers that there is something wrong in the books, when he is starting to see the seeds of corruption in the accounting books of Gotham City . . . I don't think he would have been able to do anything about it or feel anything about it unless he had seen The Batman out there." Throughout Batman's storied history, the act of Bruce Wayne donning the cape and cowl has the dark, twisted irony of also being the motivating factor in creating some of Gotham City's deadliest villains. "I think seeing The Batman was probably one of those transcendent moments in his life," said Dano. "An 'aha' moment, where you project something in you onto that figure out there, and you see some hidden piece of yourself or . . . something that you want to be. Without The Batman you would never have The Riddler, and I don't know how Edward would have survived, actually—so I think the connection is not just in the vigilante element or the political element . . . it's emotional."

As The Riddler, Nashton dons a terrifying mask and costume of his own, ready to inflict his own brand of vengeance on Gotham City's elite. Reclusive in nature, he hides out in a location with perfect views of the city's landmarks, meanwhile obsessively detailing his observations in a makeshift journal (an old accountancy ledger) . . . so far so familiar. "I think it's more similar than Bruce would like to really admit. That's why it's extremely troubling for him by the end of it, because, you know, the only difference in a lot of ways is that The Riddler follows through and kills the people," reflected Robert Pattinson. "His justice is fatal, whereas Bruce and Batman always sort of pride themselves on not killing. He somehow puts himself in a different category because of that, but I think there's such an unbelievable level of rage, and you can kind of see it toward the end of the movie. There're a lot of signs that Bruce [. . .] fears that in himself—so when The Riddler calls that out, he wants to end up punishing The Riddler because he's being a mirror to Bruce's secrets."

This version of The Riddler, one so entwined with Batman, was inspired by a notoriously horrific figure: The Zodiac Killer. "The Zodiac Killer left ciphers and eerie messages for the police and newspapers, and that kind of engagement I thought was terrifying," explained Matt Reeves. "That gave me the idea of having a Riddler who is leaving riddles and puzzles and ciphers at his crime scenes, and they're all addressed to The Batman, and Batman would have to struggle to understand why exactly he is being drawn into this." Reeves was additionally inspired by the physical descriptions of The Zodiac Killer, who too hid behind a mask. "I did a lot of reading about the power of masks—that sense of anonymity allows a kind of scary freedom of action because you're not personally accountable behind a mask. No one knows who you are. And under the right circumstances, they've found a mask can actually make some people more altruistic, and in that sense, I guess that's the flipside, the potential of the good side of Batman. But it's the other side, the unchecked power and free license of anonymity, that is so frightening."

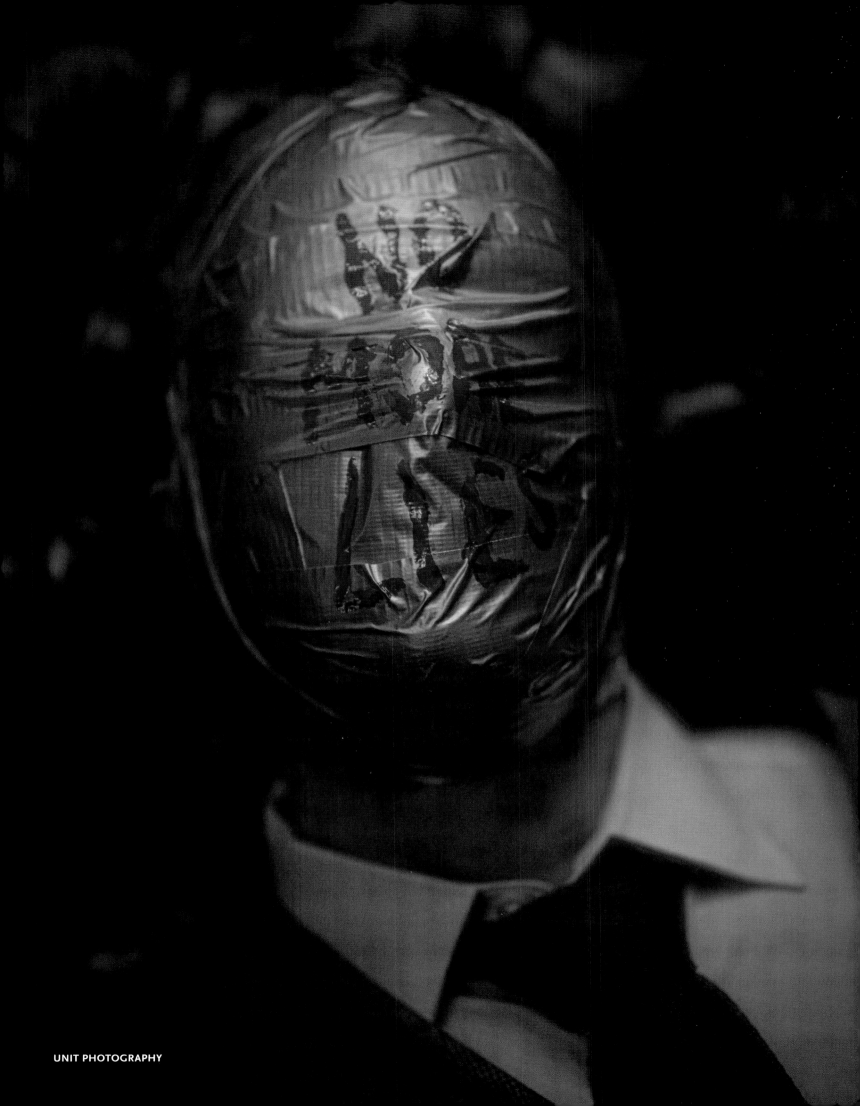

UNIT PHOTOGRAPHY

I suppose the way that I looked at it was for somebody who is probably not scary, meaning, you know—smart, numbers, puzzle obsessed, a forensic accountant. How do you take the inner pain and rage you have and make somebody else feel that? You needed something and you learn this from The Batman. You know fear, you use fear, and so this person had to find something that represented that, and of course there's other things you consider—details, the clandestine nature of it. They found this incredible mask on eBay, which is a winter combat mask, and that was definitely an "aha" moment, like, "Okay, I think that's the one," you know, 'cause there were quite a lot of different options, and Jacqueline was wonderful to work with.

With James, even just finding the way that the question mark is gonna look and the design of that was really fun to be a part of, and, frankly for me, equally as important is the costume that you see Edward Nashton in which is not in the film a lot. A guy who could just been at the desk next to you at the forensic accounting firm could be this face of horror that you know from most of the film. Something about that to me was really exciting and potentially kind of shocking or scary in its own way.

PAUL DANO

We were looking at The Zodiac Killer as a kind of obvious first choice, but that wasn't the only source. Ancient language, cuneiform, inscribed manuscript. And then we pulled on all of that and came up with our own icons, which are all drawn. Each one corresponds to the Latin alphabet.

LAURA DISHINGTON

UNIT PHOTOGRAPHY

[The Riddler's Apartment] is located across the street from the Iceberg Lounge, which is sort of the center of the action in our movie. The Riddler has picked this place, an apartment in an old Bowery sort of hotel, and he's hiding out here, developing the neck bomb, the rat cage, and all these terrible tools of terror and destruction that he's inflicting on Gotham. It's really the hub of all sorts of nefarious activities here in Gotham.

JAMES CHINLUND

The design of the space was kind of a representation of his madness. We had lots of really interesting back and forth with Paul Dano, making sure that we were on the same page in terms of representing him as a character. This simultaneously buttoned-down accountant by day, madman deep-thinker by night. It was a fine needle to thread, making sure that he didn't feel too stereotypical, but at the same time . . . scary.

JAMES CHINLUND

This is based on a real carpet tucker. This chrome finish is something that Matt very much thought should be a part of the nature of his character, and what he was doing throughout the movie. He was always trying to hide his trail and not leave evidence or fingerprints, and it's that very clinical sterile material that runs through two or three of the props.

JAMIE WILKINSON

We looked at many artists, specifically Charles
Crumb, whose journals are very much like what
you see here, with very detailed, compact writings.

LAURA DISHINGTON

Account Book

Gotham Publishing House

...OFESSION | PAID TO BANK

...not solve ...suffocating today. I SAW IT A SINGLE WORD ...desk beside me! RENEWAL! The empty ...child in that orphanage. One look inside ...whole life has been PREPARING me for ...learn the TRUTH... When I could finally ...LIES! If you want people to understand ...just give them the answers. You have to ...EM with the horrifying questions — just ...NOW NOW WHAT I MUST BECOME

Monday, July 19...

There is no escape from hell. I was born into hell. I was born into the depths of hell. There is no escape. I was born to suffer with no escape. That is my life. that is why I breathe. It will be why I live until my last breath ...child of hell. I am born into ...I know what hell is. Hell is an empty promise. An empty promise told to an empty child. An empty soul in a building full of life. Full of life with no soul. Soulless child. The screams from the orphanage I carry with me. I will forever carry them. They are my army. My ...family. In the depths of ...made you scream. They made you suffer. Is it time for a little payback? ...a little payback between neighbors. Let them into your world. Let them ...from your perspective. Let them ...darkness. Every single person in Gotham. Every man every woman every child every living creature that breathes in the decaying air of this hell hole. You have not seen hell. Not like me. Not like how I know it because I was born ...because I live it. ...Open up a little Gotham. I've a little...

...SUMMARY OF OTHER RECEIPTS

...ugh at the stupidity. The stupidity of power. But I am not the one who ...confronts, who challenges, who does ...one who will set things right. It's ...has kept me prisoner. Time has kept ...I have never left. I have ...go there. Still in the ...myself and the suffering. Time will ...go. But I will take Time back ...stand still and make Time cower ...my own. My time is coming.

We worked very closely with the graphics department. There's lots of writing and graphics that run all the way through the storytelling of the film. Matt worked for months and months with the graphics department, trying to get to the feel of this mad, crazed person, and this is all of his confessions and tormented mind.

It's all been handwritten—the reason being that Matt loved the idea of being able to see the force of the pen in the paper, almost like a typewriter making its mark.

JAMIE WILKINSON

FORM NO. WC-2 (120-0)

THE TRUTH AB
SAVAGE MURDER REPORT!
SAVAGE RETURNS
Re-Elect GIL
THE GOTHAM TIMES
THOMAS WAYNE OP
ORPHANAGE
PROMISE FULFILLED
Bruce Wayne at City Hall for Crucial Talks
WAYNE SPOTTED
Reclusive Billionaire Seen
With Mystery Women
If only I knew then... what I KNOW now...
For
Tearful Goodbye to Gotham's Thomas Wayne
Reporter

UT GOTHAM
THOMAS
Wayne
For
MURDERER
Sponsored by Friends of the Wayne Family
I
KNOW...
I know
the REAL
you...
WHO IS
THE
BAT
MAN?
CAPED CRUSADER
SEEN IN UPTOWN
Mayor Says No
the 'Batman':
GOTHAM SKIES
D OR FOE?
DON
HELL
CARRY ON
DON!

PERS
CONFI
To the Batman
FROM YOUR
SECRET
FRIEND
Whoo?
for
UCE WAYNE'S
Eyes ONLY
Wayne Manor
Mountain Drive
GOTHAM

I think it's something that Matt wrote that is really interesting, which is the riddles aren't just solace—they are also a response to the way he tortured himself with the questions of "Why?" and "Why me?" You know, "Why was I left?" "Why have I been passed around from foster home to foster home?" "What's wrong with me?" "What did I do?" "Why can't I . . ." For a person that is probably really heady and smart, Edward Nashton was tortured by the questions of his own life. And I think that's why it was so powerful when he discovered this corruption and maybe thought, "It's not my fault. It's theirs."

PAUL DANO

What does a LIAR do when he's DEAD?

Haven't a Clue?
Let's Play a Game,
just
Me and You...

I think the riddles were also a place of solace because it's probably one of the only places he could find pleasure growing up in the orphanage, which I don't think was a pleasant place. Puzzles, numbers, riddles, games—you can give yourself your own reward. You know, you see people on the subway doing their crosswords, their Sudoku, and you are engaging your mind and you get something right and it feels good. I feel like his brain, the riddles, the puzzles . . . it was one of the only ways that he could escape his situation and feel good. It was something to get lost in.

PAUL DANO

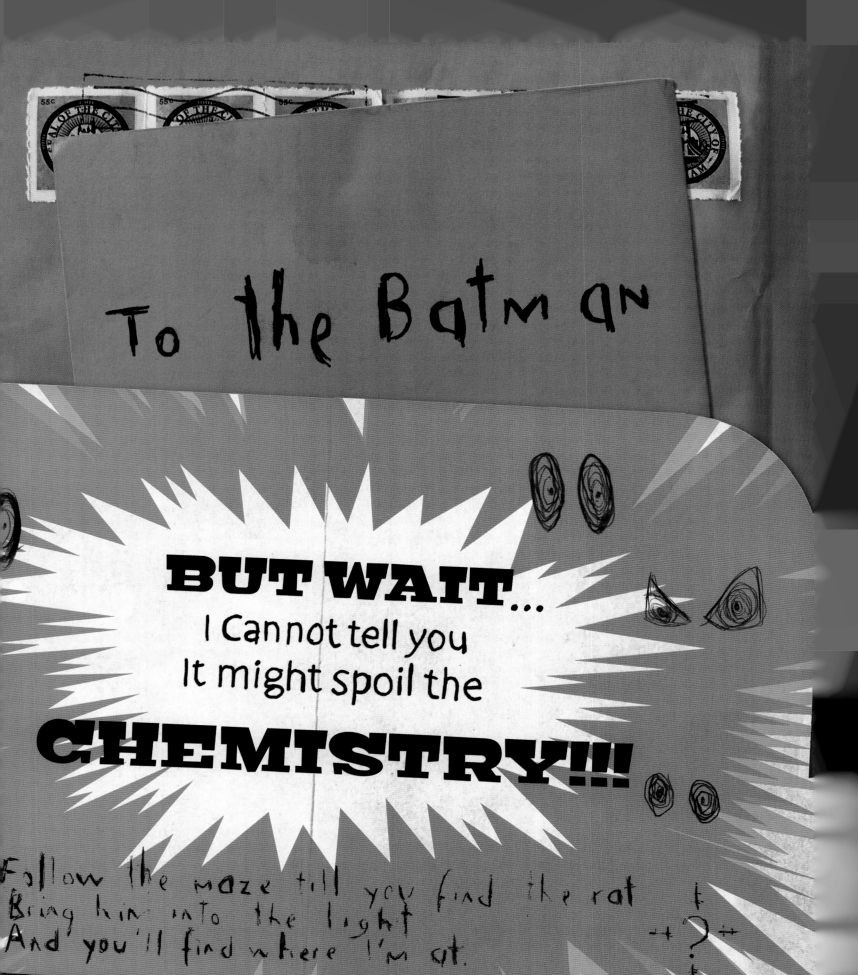

Ring... Ring...
Ring... Ring...
Ring... Ring...
Ring... Ring...
Ring... Ring...
Ring... Ring...
Ring... Ring...
Ring... Ring...
Ring... Ring...
Ring... Ring...
Ring... Ring...
Ring... Ring...
Ring... Ring...
Ring... Ring...
Ring... Ring...
Ring... Ring...

I'm just a
Phone Call Away

ANSWer.

TO THE
BatmaN

Just For You

My confession.

ANATOMY OF A SCENE
CITY HALL

With Gotham City's elite gathered for the funeral of the murdered mayor, a vehicle smashes through the doors of Gotham City Hall—plowing through the crowds and into the service, and setting The Riddler's horrifying plan into motion. In effect, it's the villain's big reveal to the world. "It was a great opportunity right at the midpoint of the movie to showcase just how realized Gotham City is," said *The Batman* producer Dylan Clark. "That set piece, for the character [of Batman], was very important—but beyond that it was an opportunity, visually, to land that our character Gotham, the city, is a character in this movie."

To shoot such an important set piece, the filmmakers built City Hall as a hybrid set—using St. George's Hall in Liverpool, England, for the exterior shots and the huge interior constructed inside the gargantuan airship hangars at Cardington Studios (also England), enhanced with additional digital extension. James Chinlund, production designer, recalled that the setup "really allowed us to explore the visual language of Gotham. We scouted quite a bit, looking for large spaces where the scene could take place. There's a major action component to the scene, so it limited places we could shoot—which, actually, for the design of the film turned out to be a tremendous advantage, because we got to design this centerpiece of the city. So we're seeing a lot of the palette, and the gothic ornament, the language of the architecture of the city come together in one big space."

For the aesthetics of City Hall, the filmmaking team took inspiration from Liverpool itself. "I think the stone that you see is more or less generated from the palette of Liverpool. But it's also a true line for Gotham. I think you're seeing, like, this heavy patina and soot, which won't be the last time you see that. I especially like playing with this patina, because it gives us a lot of contrast—which, in this low-light condition, really emerges from the shadows beautifully."

CONCEPT ART

GC-ESU

HONOR
LIEUTENANT JAMES GORDON

Established in the very first panel of the very first Batman mystery that unraveled over the pages of *Detective Comics* #27, the unlikely team of Commissioner James Gordon and The World's Greatest Detective has been Batman's longest-serving partnership—although that's not to say it's always a smooth ride. Often portrayed as a friendly but uneasy alliance, it's a case of Gordon edging a foot away from his loyalty to the Gotham City Police Department (GCPD), and Batman trying to extend trust to a relative outsider, something that feels far from natural. "Bruce doesn't really trust anyone," recounted Batman actor Robert Pattinson. "It's pretty early in their relationship and they are still really learning who each other is. It's difficult for Gordon, because

Batman is pretty set in stone that 'I do not trust anyone in the entire police department, but I trust you . . . kind of, probably about sixty percent.'"

With a stellar and award-winning career that has spanned stage and screen, including the television shows *Westworld* and *Boardwalk Empire* and the James Bond and *Hunger Games* film franchises, Jeffrey Wright grew up watching Adam West's *Batman*. "I was talking to Matt [Reeves] about these stories, and how the Batman series has evolved over time since 1939," said Wright. "It's had this eighty-year span, but he and I both kind of connected to that series. And the thing about that series is that it's a bit of a romp, pretty campy, but for me and for Matt as kids it was serious

business." Despite his fondness for the flamboyant stylings of the 1966 television show (with Neil Hamilton as its Commissioner Gordon), the actor brings a level-headed, world-weary quality to *The Batman*'s Lieutenant Jim Gordon. "The Gordon/Batman relationship in our film is Year Two, so it's not at the beginning but it's early on," recalled Wright. "Gordon is this overwhelmed everyman who's desperate to rise above the difficulties that Gotham is presenting him. He reaches out to Batman, I think, out of a level of desperation—but also a sense of admiration that he's a capable figure. He also recognizes that for some reason, not quite clear at the beginning, they're aligned. They're on the same side in terms of their perspective on the city and on what can be done in the face of the disintegration of the place." After all, this is a Batman without a Batcomputer, one who relies on the street-level intel of the likes of the GCPD. From Gordon's perspective, he sees value in working alongside The Dark Knight, but his GCPD colleagues remain largely skeptical (or downright perturbed) by the presence of a masked vigilante—one who their lieutenant has ushered onto the scene of the mayor's murder. "The curiosity that is on full display there [caused by Batman's presence] was a wonderful way of distinguishing the two of them from everyone else, that Gordon's accepting of him, accepting of the entire show," added

Wright. "That was cool because we had to earn the ease of that relationship and earn the acceptance of one another."

The Gordon presented in *The Batman* is far from the well-to-do gentleman found in *The Case of the Chemical Syndicate*. "My Gordon is very much reflective of the vision that Matt had for Gotham, but also it's reflective of the work that Robert does as Batman," said Wright. The glasses and mustache may have been a mainstay for the character's appearance ever since his debut, but, like all good comic book characters, Gordon's personality has seen substantial evolution since his first appearance. Robert Pattinson describes Wright's Jim Gordon as having "a fire in him which is a little bit different," when compared with past iterations. "What Matt's done, and what the Batman series has evolved into, is not so much a black-and-white, good-versus-evil idea, but something a little bit more nuanced," said Wright. "I don't even know if Gordon necessarily is good so much as he's desirous of being so. He's just kind of aspirational, and in some ways he's overwhelmed. He's overwhelmed by the levels of corruption and misdeeds that have overtaken the city, and he's just trying to do his best to be decent and aspiring toward some type of justice, but he's not nearly there. Whether he has the capacity to be there is another thing, but he's at least trying."

CONCEPT ART

THE BAT-SIGNAL

Eighty years since it first lit up the skies of Gotham City, The Bat-Signal is a piece of kit that has since united the efforts of both Batman and the GCPD. Primarily used by Gordon to summon Batman, the searchlight projects a bat, or the Batman insignia, up high above the cityscape. "The symbol, when it's in the sky, it scares the shit out of people," said producer Dylan Clark. "It's fear."

"As with the car, there have been many versions of this through film history," said James Chinlund, production designer for *The Batman*. "Matt and I wanted to apply the same principles that we used in the design of the car to the searchlight. So the car really shows function first, over design—the idea that Bruce crafted it with his own hands. And so, carrying that forward to the searchlight, I was really excited about the idea of 'How does this projection actually work?'" Rather than having Batman use his expertise, or Gordon using the GCPD's

already-depleted resources to commission a state-of-the-art Bat-Signal, this version took a more rudimentary approach that would fit with the film's realism. "I love the idea that Gordon came up here and took an old pair of snips and sort of snipped away at the louvers on this searchlight and created the Bat-Signal."

In reality, the prop-making team built The Bat-Signal from scratch—including a replica xenon arc bulb that would be key in making the projection work. "In the beginning of the movie, we see it fire up, and . . . we see . . . deep within its heart, we see sparks and energy and the bulb," said Chinlund. "And we see heat and water reflecting, evaporating off the hot glass. In that description it was very inspiring to me to just . . . to remember that I think what separates our movie from the others is this kind of physicality, that we're dealing with the elements—rain and heat and wind and mud, and all of these things. We really wanted to carry that forward into the design and make sure that we saw the rough edges, and we saw how this thing was made and that it was a real thing from the world that had been repurposed for the function exclusively of signaling Batman."

CONCEPT ART

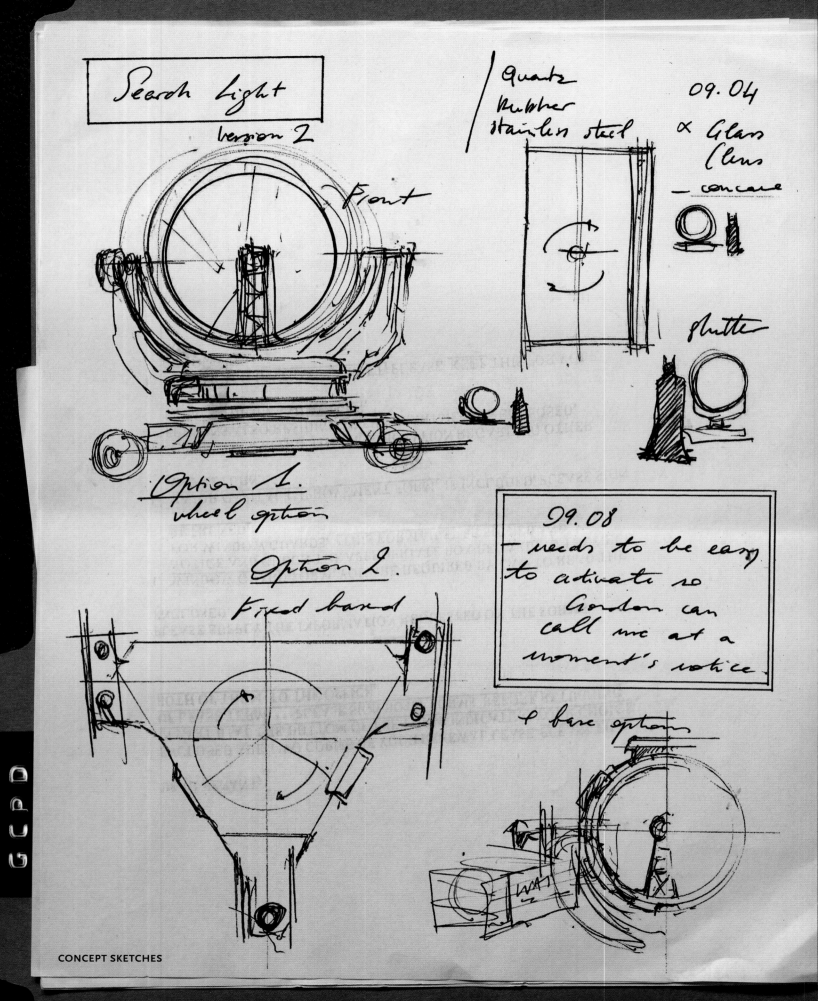

Search Light
version 2

Front

Option 1.
wheel option

Option 2.

Fixed based

Quartz
Rubber
stainless steel

09.04

α Glass
(lens
— concave

shutter

99.08
— needs to be easy
to activate so
Gordon can
call me at a
moment's notice

& base options

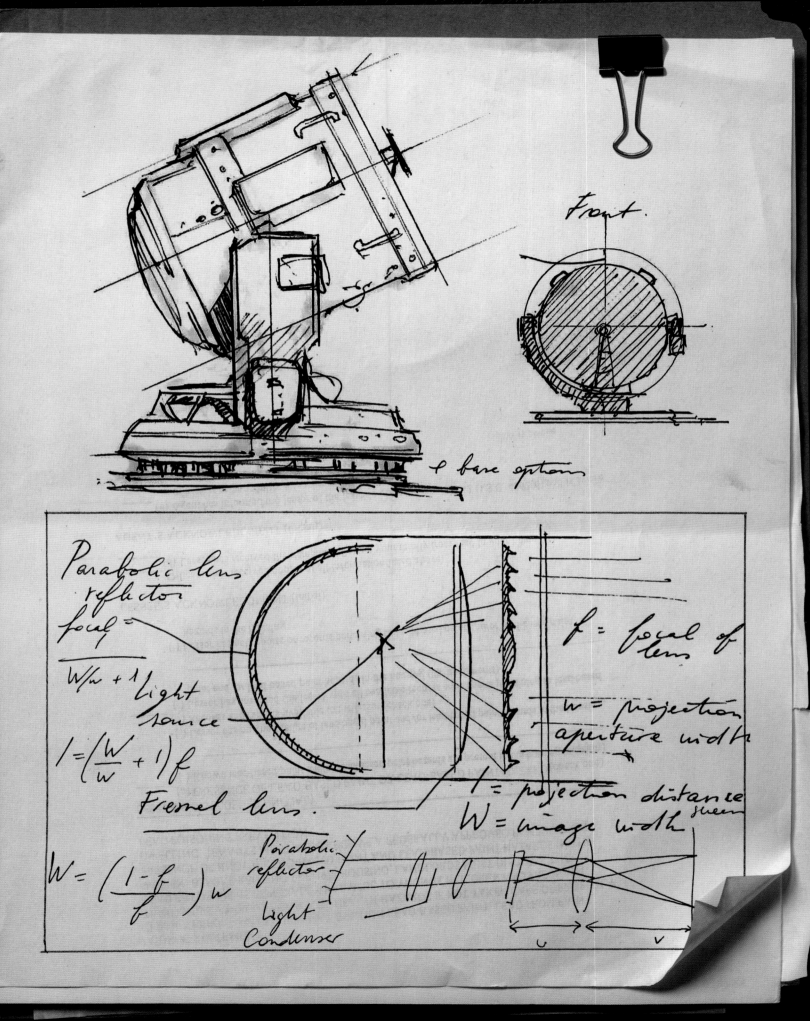

Front.

& base options

Parabolic lens
reflector

$$focal = \frac{}{W/w + 1}$$

Light
source

$$1 = \left(\frac{W}{w} + 1\right) f$$

Fresnel lens.

$$W = \left(\frac{1-f}{f}\right) w$$

Parabolic
reflector

Light
Condenser

f = focal of lens f

w = projection aperture width

1 = projection distance

W = image width

screen

CONCEPT ART

ANATOMY OF A SCENE
ESCAPE FROM GCPD

When the atmosphere at GCPD Headquarters turns hostile, Batman is required to make a hasty escape out of the building. With the police in pursuit, Batman first uses his grappling hook to traverse up the station's main stairwell—launching himself to the very top of the building before the bewildered cops' eyes. It was filmed in the Lethaby Building at Central Saint Martins in London, England, the former arts college becoming home to the Gotham City Police Department—with its combination of Victorian and industrial architecture providing the perfect look for the severely underfunded service. "Gotham is suffering under the decay and corruption of the Don Mitchell administration, so we're hoping that this building and its amazing patina and layers will show you just how sort of backward the Gotham Police Department is," said James Chinlund. "We're really trying to show the layering, the intensity Gotham PD is putting into this, and also just the feeling of them being completely overwhelmed by the crime and corruption in the city. We're really hoping to hit you in the face with the idea that they'll never be able to dig out from under the weight of the immensity of the corruption and crime in Gotham."

Once he's made his way to the building's roof (scenes of which were shot at the very top of the Liver Building in Liverpool, England), Batman needs a way out—and fast. By quickly reconnecting and adjusting a series of elements on his existing cape, the vigilante suddenly has a working wingsuit. "Whereas in the previous Batman films you have it kind of miraculously turning into a glider, it doesn't quite feel that realistic," said Batsuit designer Glyn Dillon. "Matt really wanted it to feel like Bruce Wayne has worked out a way of making this thing that he wears on his back all the time have some practical use." Producer Dylan Clark saw the chance to combine the practical with on-screen spectacle. "When you see footage of the wingsuit jumpers, it just looks incredible," he began, "You've not really seen it in a city, and you've certainly not seen it with an iconic character running away from the cops in the night, crashing to the streets below. It always has to come out of character— why is he actually putting this into his arsenal? And if you can't answer that then you're in trouble."

With the costume locked in, it was now down to director of photography Greig Fraser to work out how to shoot Batman's wingsuit as it takes flight—off the side of GCPD Headquarters, hurtling through the air before the hero crashes down onto the streets of Gotham City. While the final Batman wingsuit was inspired by how real-world ones look and move, they are often filmed in flight using dynamic, handheld cameras. Fraser explained that "the way that those things are done is with small cameras and they're not very cinematic, but they're very exciting. So we couldn't change the style of our movie to suit that wingsuit. It had to flow through, and it had to feel like it was all integrated. It was a headache, but it was an exciting headache."

When we arrived at the kind of subtly retro version of the police, it was the first kind of strong foundation I'd seen for how to build up the Gotham world that we wanted.

JACQUELINE DURRAN

BATMAN: YEAR ONE   David Mazzucchelli (pencils & inks)

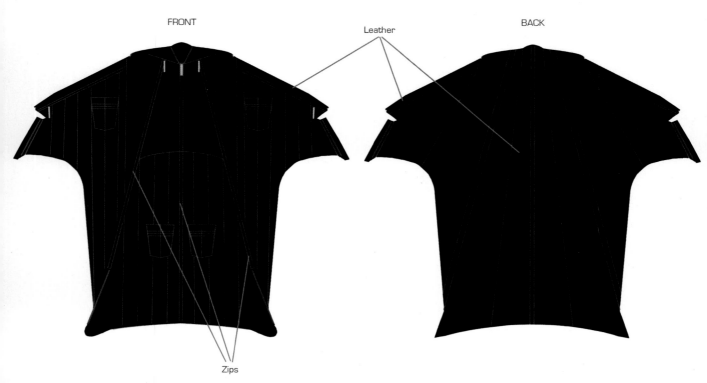

FRONT

Leather

BACK

Zips

CONCEPT SKETCH

Loose webbing

Lacing detail that matches the suit

CONCEPT ART

RETRIBUTION
SELINA KYLE

Back in 2019, the actress Zoë Kravitz heard rumblings that a search for a new Catwoman was under way, so she threw her hat into the ring. "When I got this part I was floored, and then when the news came out I, to this day, not even on my birthday, have never received so many phone calls and text messages," recalled Kravitz. "That was when it hit me—this isn't just big to me, this is just a big deal. Eartha Kitt and Michelle Pfeiffer and Halle Berry, everybody. It's an honor to be in that group of people." Off the back of critical acclaim for her performance in the HBO television series *Big Little Lies*, along with huge commercial success in the *Fantastic Beasts* and *Divergent* franchises, Kravitz found herself taking on the role of one of comic book fandom's most beloved and exciting characters: Selina Kyle—aka Catwoman. "There were times when I really had to actually step away from that, because I think the pressure for it to be iconic, or to compare myself to those other incredible actresses, I think that's really dangerous," continued Kravitz. "Especially because this story is so specific, I really wanted it to feel character-driven, and I wanted it to feel like it was coming from the inside, an internal thing, not an external thing. It is, in a way, about how she looks and moves—but it's really about her spirit, and that was what I really wanted to focus on. I didn't want to get trapped in trying to make something iconic or sexy. I really wanted it to be a story about a woman who survived a hell of a life and is trying to figure out what to do next."

Under the initial guise of the Cat, the jewel thief and femme fatale Selina Kyle first crossed paths with the Caped Crusader in the comic *Batman* #1 (1940). Over the years, Catwoman has been considered both a trusted ally and a ruthless antagonist of Batman, but it's often been the character's questionable morals that have made Selina such an enduring comic book icon. "I wouldn't call Selina a villain," offered Kravitz, "but I think even some of the other villains in the story, they all have really interesting valid points, and I think that's what's so wonderful about this world. The exploration of the gray area." While the Selina Kyle we meet in *The Batman* is yet to take on the identity of Catwoman, the character still operates with a familiarly dubious morality—working a series of underground jobs in the seedy, dilapidated downtown Gotham City, while secretly plotting to avenge her mother. When a horrible tragedy happens close to home, it further fuels Selina's personal vendetta against some of the city's most powerful figures. "What was really important to me is that Selina didn't come off as a victim, because she comes from a really troubled past, and I think there can be a little bit of a trap with female characters who come from troubled pasts, or are vengeful in some way where they feel like a victim," Kravitz said. "I really found a character who was more than just a sidekick or more than just a good-looking girl in a tight outfit. This is a real person who has struggled a lot, and I admire her and feel for her." Matt Reeves sought to bestow Selina Kyle with the complexity that went above the simple "femme fatale" trope. "Selina's a survivor. She had to survive on the streets, and she actually lived for part of her childhood in the Gotham Orphanage, just like The Riddler. And so the story's very much about class as well, and about the luxury of being able to choose to become a vigilante, versus somebody who simply has to find a way to survive in the way that Selina does."

UNIT PHOTOGRAPHY

BATMAN: YEAR ONE   David Mazzucchelli (pencils & inks)

The most significant comic was *Year One*. That also formed one of the keystones in the creation. It was particularly important for me with Selina, because we're not in the Catwoman world yet. We're pre-Catwoman. So *Year One* was very important in knowing what that looked like.

JACQUELINE DURRAN

UNIT PHOTOGRAPHY

For the filmmaking team, one of the most important influences on this iteration of Selina Kyle was Frank Miller and David Mazzucchelli's *Batman: Year One*, which depicts the future Catwoman as a force to be reckoned with, and one who appears hardened by the experiences that she has undergone. "That Selina Kyle is the savior for the ill-treated, the forgotten, the people who have not had anybody looking after them," said *The Batman* producer Dylan Clark. "She's that person in the toughest part of the city who brings in the strays to make sure they're okay. She's the opposite of the damsel in distress. She's also very complicated. You don't quite know exactly where her loyalty or her allegiance lies, but she's there to fight for those

who need help." Taking on the role of the resilient, resourceful, and agile Selina Kyle meant that Kravitz needed to undergo an intense training regime. Having been taught tae kwon do by supervising stunt coordinator Rob Alonzo since she was a child, Kravitz had a sense of what to expect. "He's really dedicated to it feeling real, it feeling messy, it feeling accurate. We're not doing things that don't feel possible; I'm not wearing shoes I couldn't walk in. If I couldn't pick somebody up, I won't do it. He's really concerned about it feeling grounded and real, and being motivated by emotion. But the first couple months of training—it was intense. I've never felt so strong in my life, and so that's been transformative."

SELINA'S
MOTORBIKE

CONCEPT ART

This is an amazing bike that is built on a BMW body, and a beautiful piece of design by Cherry Custom Motorcycles. We saw this design early on and this had such an amazing, aggressive look that we felt like it really fit beautifully for Selina. This is generation one of Selina becoming Catwoman, and finding her identity.

We had actually landed on the design of the bike before Zoë was cast, so we had no idea if it would fit her. So it was an amazing thing the first day she walked up and slid onto the bike, and it was like Cinderella's slippers because, amazingly, it's a perfect fit.

The important thing was that you see that Selina has been working out on this bike, she's been learning, learning her abilities as a rider, and also she's been through various scrapes and bangs. She doesn't have all the resources in the world—she's cobbled this bike together from parts. She's at the beginning of her journey too, and nothing's perfect.

JAMES CHINLUND

Matt and I were super inspired by some of the films of Wong Kar-wai
early on—textures and patterns and things like that, we loved playing
with some of those things. There's sort of a romantic sort of palette
in some of Wong Kar-wai's movies that we loved. But also the life of
this part of the city, which is the red light district, we felt like letting
in a bit more color. There's neon, a lot of color from the light in the
street. Our world is so dark and so sort of like grim in a lot of places
that we were looking for places where we could let some color pop.

JAMES CHINLUND

LOCATION
SELINA'S APARTMENT

BATMAN: YEAR ONE David Mazzucchelli (pencils & inks)

We tried to think about what a woman of Selina's history and current work situation, where she would find herself in the city. We also drew a lot of inspiration from the *Year One* comic. In that comic, Selina is living in the red-light district. So we loved that and tried to use that as an inspiration for her neighborhood.

[Selina's apartment is] located in the East End of Gotham, in the red-light district. She lives on top of an old burlesque theater called The East End. This is where she lives with her roommate, Anika. And that's where we find her.

JAMES CHINLUND

CONCEPT ART

There's some physical requirements to this set. She's sort of living this double life. She's hiding sort of her identity from Anika, her roommate.

In her closet, for example, there's a secret wall on the back of the closet where all her weapons and cat burglarizing tools are rigged, and disguises and things like that. This is really the epicenter of her secret life as a cat burglar, so we're seeing lots of evidence of her experiments with safecracking. We see all her extender rigs and her climbing equipment, disguises and weapons development. So we're seeing the interior world of Selina in this room.

There's a scene where they track through the apartment, and she jumps out the window dressed as Catwoman and goes to her motorcycle below. So that was the physical requirement of the set—that, in one shot, we could take her from the door to the window and down to the garage below . . . which led us to being elevated.

JAMES CHINLUND

As with Batman, we're seeing her build her character, so representing in her apartment the development of her tools and her weapons. Learning her craft, safe-cracking, rope climbing, and all this sort of stuff that we really were hoping that you would feel as you move through her place.

JAMES CHINLUND

BATMAN: YEAR ONE
David Mazzucchelli (pencils & inks)

This costume isn't a catsuit. Selina isn't Catwoman yet, and so that was one of the things that made it a challenge, because it needed to be a suit that was in the real world, from the real world. She's not Catwoman yet, so you can't go the full way of making the fully-fledged catsuit. You're somewhere between the two, but you need to make it catsuit enough that it registers the fact that she's going to turn into Catwoman.

JACQUELINE DURRAN

Specifically with the jumpsuit, it's like a leather jacket. How do you reinvent that? How do you make it new? How do you make it feel like its own thing? It was very important that it felt practical. It's not some fashion thing—she wears it because she rides a bike. Then we talked about different shapes and silhouettes and all of that. The lighting, too—we wanted some parts that felt shiny just to catch the light.

The detail on the suit is amazing. There's areas that have been patched up and have different kinds of leather and scratches. You can just tell she's worn this thing to shit, which I love. It feels very feminine and very sexy, but still at the same time practical.

The catsuit of this film is what she's wearing to bike around in—it's kind of alluding to what Catwoman will be. The idea of having this wind mask that is just a little hint of ears, like the hat just kind of happened to fall that way.

ZOË KRAVITZ

MORPHING INTO CATWOMAN

In addition to the physical regime undertaken by Zoë Kravitz to prepare for the more action-packed sequences, the journey of retribution undertaken by Selina Kyle in *The Batman* required the actress to adopt a range of tailored appearances and personalities to move seamlessly among both Gotham's most downtrodden and its elite. "Zoë Kravitz has actually ended up with four different looks from a hair and makeup perspective in this film," revealed hair designer Zoe Tahir (*Justice League*, *Ready Player One*, *Spectre*). "We spent a lot of time in the begin-

ning playing around with wigs, different lengths, shapes, colors, styles, and it became quite apparent quite early on what was not going to work. And then, as costumes became established, and because of the storyline, and what she was doing, where she was going, how she was presenting herself, it became quite clear what looks would work for what moment."

Under the guise of a server at one of Gotham City's most notorious nightclubs, the Iceberg Lounge, there was a fantastic opportunity to connect Selina's style with an iconic comic book look. "She's a waitress, she's at a club, she has to dress like this, and we still got to have some really fun fashion moments," said Kravitz. "I really think the way this began was probably in reference to the *Year One* comic, where Selina has this really great two-piece outfit, and we wanted to re-create that and slowly get to that place." Through the film's unfolding narrative, Selina's costumes were able to illustrate the character's journey toward eventually becoming more aligned with the Selina Kyle and Catwoman fans have become so familiar with.

BATMAN: THE LONG HALLOWEEN
Tim Sale (pencils & inks) and Gregory Wright (colors)

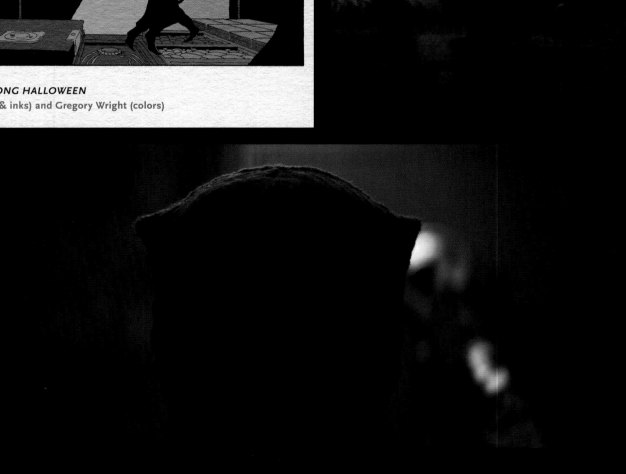

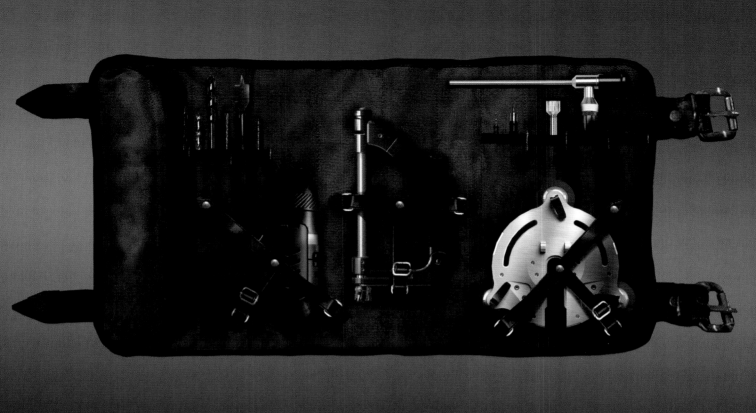

ANATOMY OF A SCENE
THE FIRST ENCOUNTER

From its very conception in 1940, at the heart of the Batman/Catwoman dynamic has been a continual cat-and-mouse game. "Cat-and-mouse is a great way to describe it. I think there's a love-hate thing, and I think the line between love and hate is very thin," said Zoë Kravitz. "There's a really deep soul connection, even though they see things differently and they come from very different backgrounds. I think that they are actually fighting for the same thing and they're both people who really believe in justice. Their idea of what justice is might be a little bit different, but they're both

BATMAN: THE LONG HALLOWEEN
Tim Sale (pencils & inks) and Gregory Wright (colors)

CATWOMAN!

How many of her lives has she used up since this whole nightmare began?

BATMAN: THE LONG HALLOWEEN Tim Sale (pencils & inks) and Gregory Wright (colors)

CONCEPT ART

The keyhole shape is an important aspect in the design that's reflected in the bridge that is going to be living in extension out there. So it's sort of like this idea that this circle runs all the through the set and leads us out to the bridge. Again, just doing everything we can to emphasize, reinforce the feeling that we're inside this massive structure.

JAMES CHINLUND

POWER

FALCONE & THE PENGUIN

The Tricorner Bridge of Gotham City is home to some of the city's most scrupulous figures, conducting criminal activity while going either unnoticed by the GCPD or flat-out unreported due to certain officers' complicity. Not only did the bridge play an important part in Gotham City's design, from its subway maps to its official seals, but the structure itself had an important narrative and geographical role—housing three of *The Batman*'s key, nefarious hangout spots inside the bridge itself. "We were excited about building a world for Gotham City that is entirely our own,

and something the world has never seen before," said production designer James Chinlund. "We had to find a way of stitching together the Iceberg Lounge, the 44 Below, and Falcone's Loft all within a similar sort of area. So when we started playing around with this bridge idea, it seemed like a great way." With the layering of three of Gotham City's landmarks, it also symbolized an epic power struggle taking place in the city's darkest corner, between a mysterious crime lord and a man waiting with dwindling patience to take the throne . . .

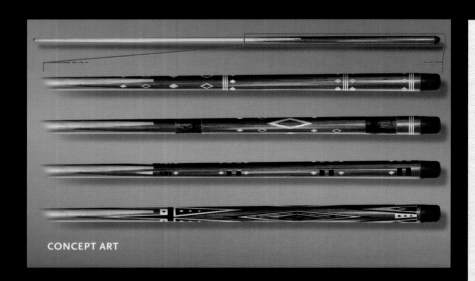

CONCEPT ART

We were keying off the bronze of the bridge. There's a verdigris in the bronze and so we felt like a teal would just be an exciting thing to play with. Also, we knew we would be picking up the color of the pool table, so we figured just to embrace it.

JAMES CHINLUND

BATMAN: THE LONG HALLOWEEN
Tim Sale (pencils & inks) and Gregory Wright (colors)

CARMINE FALCONE

At the very top of the Tricorner Bridge, in what would have once been the Department of Tolls and Bridges for the City of Gotham, resides the reclusive mafia boss Carmine Falcone. Introduced to readers in Miller and Mazzucchelli's *Year One*, Falcone is a man with Gotham-wide influence over the city's officials, services, and industries—with a key role to play in *The Long Halloween*, and first portrayed on-screen by actor Tom Wilkinson in *Batman Begins*. "I'm definitely a Batman fan," began John Turturro, who would inhabit the role for *The Batman*. A New York native, Turturro joins the cast as a hugely respected, award-winning actor, director, writer, and producer—whose work spans film, television, and theater, and who has collaborated with the likes of Spike Lee (*Do the Right Thing*), the Coen brothers (*Miller's Crossing, The Big Lebowski, O Brother, Where Art Thou?*) and Ridley Scott (*Exodus: Gods and*

Kings). "When I was a kid, I used to read the comics, and I was actually a big Zorro fan—which inspired Batman." The script's noir stylings were of particular interest to film aficionado Turturro, so he met with the filmmakers to discuss the look and feel of such a wealthy, connected yet reserved individual. "We really re-created the character straight from the comic book," said *The Batman* makeup designer Naomi Donne (*Cruella, Murder on the Orient Express* [2017]). "He had the thin mustache, and he has these scars on his face that we made. It was a small prosthetic that we applied all the time, and it was a really good link with Catwoman." With minimalistic, handsome suits made bespoke in London's Savile Row, costume designer Jacqueline Durran added that they wanted to echo the suggestion that "many of the most powerful people in the world are not ones who call attention to themselves. They kind of sit back and stay in the shadows."

With its eagle's nest view across Gotham City, it was important to establish a unique setting for Falcone not only to be holed up in for his own safety, but to further the idea of his control and manipulation over its citizens. "The inspiration for the set was Robert Moses, who is a notorious figure in the history of New York," revealed production designer James Chinlund.

"He ran something called the Triborough Commission, and basically he was responsible for masterminding all these road projects throughout the city. Legend has it that his office was beneath a toll plaza in the bridge, and so as the money flowed in from the tolls it went right through a tube into his office. I always thought that was an amazing idea for this villain." As with the Iceberg Lounge and the 44 Below underneath it, Falcone's shoreline loft is a mix of plush lifestyle (an intricate, personalized pool table and cues, chester-field sofas, expensive artwork) and artifacts from Gotham City's industrial past—including a series of eye-catching circular windows for watching over the city. For the filmmakers, it allowed for a unique source of light during one of the movie's most dramatic sequences. "When the power is out there are cars that are moving along, so we're getting this incredible light," said James Chinlund, "and that goes back to some of those inspirations from the comics, the shafted light. We see the light from the headlights of the cars, one of the only things that's going to be illuminating this room, so you'll get these staccato wipes of light in the space, which just felt like a really cool backdrop for a fight."

THE ICEBERG LOUNGE & THE 44 BELOW

Synonymous with The Penguin across the character's many appearances, the Iceberg Lounge is typically one of Gotham City's trendiest hotspots—in addition to being a front for the criminal dealings of Cobblepot and his cronies. "We were trying to figure out how to present that in a grounded way in our world, so we were playing with the idea of this fish company that occupied this space in the anchorage of the Tricorner Bridge," said production designer James Chinlund. It was originally more extravagant in design, with a river flowing through the club, but Chinlund and his team eventually settled on taking inspiration from the bridge's industrial past—once again thinking practically about what the structure would actually lend itself to visually. "When we designed the space we weren't quite sure what the [dancers'] performance was going to be, and so the chutes that came down from the factory above were the genesis of the idea," continued Chinlund. "We started organizing the space around that. As the dancers started materializing and we started exploring what the performance would be, we realized what a perfect place for a pole. And then the performer was actually using the chute and sort of disappearing up into the chute and reappearing, so it was just a really nice piece of serendipity."

As light floods through the dance floor, it pierces through the grates and into a secret club in the bowels of the bridge: the 44 Below—a speakeasy-like arrangement for Gotham City's underworld to conduct business in private. "The genesis was trying to tell the story of the layering. The Penguin sitting above the club, the dance floor level of the club itself, and then the 44 Below way down in the basement. I loved the idea of trying to connect those spaces visually, so The Penguin is looking down on the dance floor." With the 44 Below situated under the old factory, remnants of its production line such as fish chutes and load-bearing steel are intertwined with luxurious suede seating and a central ice sculpture. The attention to set detail, and desire to continue the momentum of story through location, also flowed through to the props. Zoë Kravitz recalled, "They have all these little stations where all the showgirls have their mirrors and their makeup and their stuff, and I would look at every individual mirror and everyone had their own story. There were love notes left, there were pregnancy tests, there were empty bottles of whiskey, there were notes, there were lipsticks, there were broken eyeliner pencils . . . it was just alive, and that's the kind of detail that makes Gotham feel so real and gritty."

THE PENGUIN

Occupying two-thirds of the space within the Tricorner Bridge is club owner and crime boss-in-waiting Oswald Cobblepot, or "Oz," as he prefers to be known— however, there's another nickname he has acquired in the beginnings of his career, one that he finds far more undesirable: The Penguin. "I wanted to see a Batman film that was not an origin tale, but was about his early days. But that meant a lot of the char- acters who are the Rogues Gallery characters *would be* in their origin phases," said Matt Reeves. "So we have a Selina Kyle who's not yet Catwoman, but you can see all of the pieces. And we have a Penguin who's not yet the kingpin, but you can see the seeds of that as well. In the comics, what's so interesting and fun is that many of those characters, ironically, are inspired by the presence of this masked vigilante. And they become their own alter-egos of themselves in this kind of darker way. So there's a real dialogue between Batman and the Rogues Gallery."

In the 1942 caper "Crime's Early Bird," Batman encountered an unusual adversary—a portly gentle- man who wears a top hat and monocle, with an arsenal of umbrellas that were reconfigured into gimmicky weapons. The *Detective Comics* #67 version of The Penguin had a bird-influenced appearance along with an aristocratic air about him that seemed to stick,

especially with one of the most memorable uses of the character—in the 1966 *Batman* TV series, where a chain-smoking, loudly quacking Penguin (played by Burgess Meredith) took glee in trying to outsmart the Dynamic Duo. More than a quarter of a century later, Tim Burton's *Batman Returns* would put a dark, twisted spin on Cobblepot, with Danny DeVito play- ing a deformed, marginalized Penguin who has long watched the world from afar. It may have taken a further thirty years for The Penguin's third cinematic outing, but with that wait comes another innovative take on the character. "I was aware of Matt's work from *Cloverfield* and on the *Apes* films, and Matt's an extraordinary director," said actor Colin Farrell. "I read the script and the script was extraordinary. He had an incredible depth to it, and an incredible sense of lone- liness and isolation. Every single character, whether it was articulated or not, seemed to be imbued with a sense of backstory and a sense of subtext and a kind of deep emotional and psychological undercurrent."

When the eagerly anticipated first trailer for *The Batman* was unveiled at DC FanDome in 2020, fans were astonished by the reveal of The Penguin—in total disbelief that the character was being played by a completely unrecognizable Colin Farrell. Under layers of expertly applied prosthetics and makeup, even the actor's costars were bamboozled on set. Zoë Kravitz recalled, "He walked right up to me, and I was looking for Colin in there and I couldn't see him. Still to this day, actually, 'cause I've only met Colin a few times outside of this film, I feel like I don't know Colin Farrell. I know The Penguin." Developing such a

shocking visual transformation required the expertise of prosthetic makeup designer Mike Marino and prosthetic artist Mike Fontaine. Having worked together for more than ten years, they were both mentored by legendary makeup artist Dick Smith, and between them they have lent their craft to films such as *The Many Saints of Newark*, *The Irishman*, *Joker*, and many more. "Matt [Reeves] had some ideas on what he wanted The Penguin to be," recounted Marino. "He wanted something that was a little pathetic and a little sympathetic. He was referencing Fredo from *The God-father*, and the look of Bob Hoskins. I kind of sculpted Fredo's brow onto Colin as close as I could, and then I started tweaking it from there. It just developed into this strange mob kind of character and a scarred-up, grizzled, heavy guy with maybe an insecurity."

The initial application of the extensive prosthetics work took between three and four and a half hours, piecing together each of the individual components— cheeks, nose, earlobes . . . the list goes on. "Once the pieces are glued on, then we start painting it, airbrushing different tones and colors and ambers and reds and all these things to match his skin tone as close as possible," said Marino. "Some of the things that I wanted to get rid of were some of the signature things

on Colin Farrell, like his eyebrows. I created this shape of his eyebrow like a penguin. And if you look on the side of his profile, I threw in a little subliminal bird beak, the way his nose is shaped, 'cause it looks like a chipped-up scar. So, it looks like a penguin beak from the side." For Farrell, the dramatic physical transformation fed into his understanding of the character. "You look at his face and you see some scars," he recalled. "It was fun creating a backstory for every single mark and every single issue that he has, 'cause there's a wealth of a kind of information, of personal history that one can design. You would hope that from thinking about it, even subtextually or unconsciously, this information finds its way into the character and onto the screen—but certainly lends itself to much more road." In addition to influencing a change in the actor's natural gait and movement, the prosthetics inspired a particular way of speaking. "Marino recorded a little piece of me in the makeup," began Farrell. "I didn't feel like I was ready, but he asked me a few questions and I answered them. And then when I saw it back, I thought, 'That sounds good,' because my voice actually sounds different. The timbre of it sounds different. It sounds like it's in a different place. It sounds heavier. It sounds like it's struggling a bit more."

I poured over all the comic books. I used to love Burgess Meredith as The Penguin, and Danny DeVito, obviously, everyone knows. But I looked at everything that I thought looked interesting as The Penguin. I tried to incorporate some of the things from the comics, but I think we're reinventing, in a sense, what The Penguin is—especially if he works underground as a gangster. I think there are many elements that you could relate to the comic book illustrations over the years. You'll find pieces of things in his face which may relate to the comics.

MIKE MARINO

The thing that we took for The Penguin [from the comics] is the color purple. So there's a little bit of purple sprinkled in, but we didn't want to make it too heavy or too obvious. It's there, but it wasn't the overriding thing.

   I was looking at a lot of pictures of gangsters through time, particularly the forties and the eighties. We ended up with a kind of amalgamation of those two periods.

JACQUELINE DURRAN

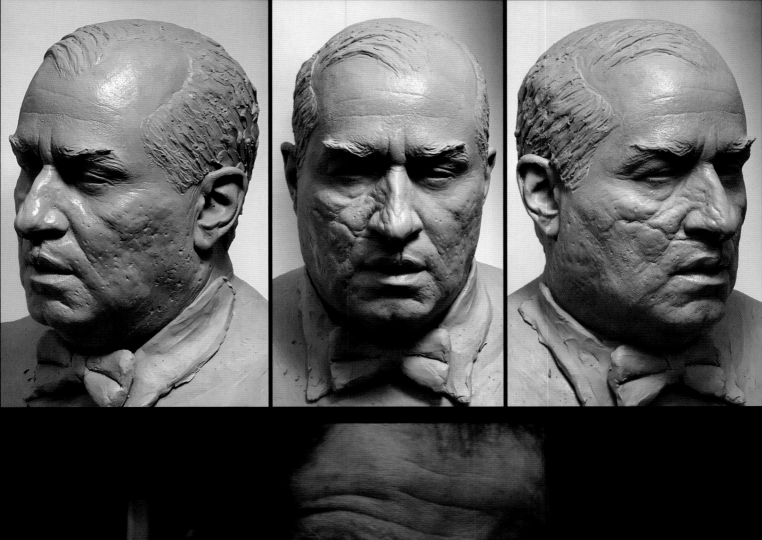

Gotham Renewal Corporation is sort of like the big umbrella of corruption in Gotham, and there's subsidiaries of that. Gotham Recycling is a subsidiary of Gotham Renewal, and they are using the recycling trucks to help them distribute the drugs around the city. It's the perfect cover because they can throw them into the dumpsters, and then the trucks distribute them throughout the town.

JAMES CHINLUND

CONCEPT ART

THE BATMOBILE & THE PENGUIN CAR CHASE

Tracking down The Penguin's thugs to a deserted warehouse on Gotham City's waterfront, Batman uncovers a secret drug lab that is producing the deadly "Drops"— a designer drug that has made waves through the city, and an operation that was considered obsolete since the death of the previous mob boss, Salvatore Maroni. As a gunfight breaks out, Batman is seemingly cornered by The Penguin and his goons, but suddenly a "guttural, terrifyingly loud engine growls"—the reveal of The Batmobile, before a high-octane chase through the streets of Gotham City begins. "The chase in this movie is one of the most intense chase scenes I've ever seen," said production designer James Chinlund. "The general thrust of the chase, the idea that Batman is relentlessly pursuing The Penguin, is the ethos of the car, and that has been there from Day One. In Matt's mind, the shape of the chase is that Batman will just not stop. The Penguin is running, and he just can't believe how relentless this pursuit is in spite of all his attempts to evade him."

CONCEPT ART

Batman is The World's Greatest Detective. He follows The Penguin and some dirty cops back to this spot from The Penguin's club, the Iceberg Lounge.

JAMES CHINLUND

VR TO SCREEN

I've always found the previs aspect of the filmmaking process to be challenging. I have to find a personal connection to where the camera goes, and it's hard to explore a virtual space without being able to walk right into it. With *The Batman*, the opportunity finally happened. James Chinlund designed the sets in VR, so we were able to walk those sets before they were ever built. The experience was amazing. I could look for shots and act out what I had written. And we could figure out on the spot how to change a set based on exploring the space together.

MATT REEVES

GROCERY
· MEAT · COFFEE

GOTHA M

CONCEPT ART

DESPAIR GOTHAM CITY

Throughout the Batman films, the look and feel of Gotham City has been one of the most explicit ways for filmmakers to visualize their take on the franchise, creating an individual view on and aesthetic for the world that reflects the inner emotions of their particular interpretation of Batman himself. For *The Batman*, Matt Reeves recognized the importance of Gotham in the story. "As the Riddler's crimes allude to the history of corruption in Gotham, the idea of the presence of that place as a character is critical," Reeves said. He envisioned a Gotham City that was altogether familiar yet excitingly new, explaining, "What we wanted to do was shoot in real cities with gothic architecture, and on our beautifully built gothic sets, and then use convincing CGI to extend and add in the more modern city structures and skyscrapers, so that you look at it all and go, 'Wow, I've never been to that city, but it looks like a completely believable American metropolis—that must be the real Gotham.'" For well-informed fans there are plenty of nods to familiar Batman and DC Comics locations and landmarks, but the importance was on creating a Gotham City that looked stunning but felt unpredictable and dangerous. "There's something about it, the combination of these stunningly beautiful buildings just surrounded by decay and grime," remarked Robert Pattinson. "It's like how Bruce sees the city. It's like his perception of the whole thing—the city used to be great, and now it's just been totally taken over." Colin Farrell echoed this, revealing that "it feels like a place of spiritual corruption in a way, and corruption is one of the key elements, key narrative elements in this story: political corruption, environmental corruption."

Inspired by America's rust belt, Matt Reeves said that "the idea is this place has really not served its people well. This is a place of just tremendous corruption. And its best days seem well behind it." Production designer James Chinlund added. "Over the

years, there have been stops, starts, sort of renewal projects, and development projects that've stalled. So what that allowed us to do is create these kinds of rusting hulks where you saw massive towers that were incomplete. I love the way those sorts of skeletal shapes in the skyline would marry with the Gothic shapes and allow us to create a world that felt simultaneously modern, but not shiny and new. So I think we really leaned into the idea that there were a lot of failed attempts, and you could see those representations of the failure of the system in the skyline itself."

Expanding on their experience of working together on the *Apes* films, Matt Reeves, Dylan Clark, James Chinlund, and VFX supervisor Dan Lemmon began working out how to bring their Gotham City to life. "We bring people with us that believe in our philosophy," said Clark. "I think what's important to me is that we don't take shortcuts. We choose ambitious, challenging scenes and then we try to figure out how to do them realistically, but also bring a freshness to them. It's a combination of both getting things practically and finding ways to incorporate visual effects in a smart way. But it's always done through how you serve the character's story that we're watching unfold." They started the process by scouring US-based locations—including New York, Chicago, and Pittsburgh. However, with the film shoot taking place in the UK, their attention turned to some of the country's most historic architecture. "Once I started scouting and looking around Manchester, Liverpool, and Glasgow, we started to realize that there's a language there that is unique," said Chinlund. "There's sort of a decayed Gothic layer that we just don't have in the States, and it was a real opportunity for us to combine practical set builds, some Chicago location work, and then a bunch of this amazing, rich tapestry of architecture from the UK—and try to weave all that into an American city that you've never seen before." Taking the

basic structure of buildings, the team expanded upon the actual buildings with more drastic visual effects—ensuring that the textures of old were expanded upon with convincing modern architecture. "When you're doing the visual effects, CG surfaces that are easier are steel or glass," said Reeves. "Photographically, by shooting something that's real, you have tremendous reference for how to light the other objects you'll be putting in there." Chinlund added, "The truth is that the way I design, I like to write out a set of rules for the world. I feel like I need a road map as I move forward. And so thinking about the effects of corruption and crime, and obviously a bit of climate change too, on the city; what that would look like, helped us generate the visual rules that would guide us going forward."

Establishing scale was an important factor in presenting a feasible Gotham, with several scenes depicting character movement through a bustling city during Halloween. In order to get a feel for what

inhabiting Gotham City might be like, the filmmakers opted to use virtual reality (VR) technology. "I'm a huge advocate for virtual reality," said director of photography Greig Fraser. "To be able to sort of walk into a set virtually, as if you were there, and make decisions about it before a single piece of construction has gone ahead. You're able, then, to better foresee the problems that occur." Chinlund teamed up with visual effects art director Tad Davis, the two having previously worked together on the live-action retelling of *The Lion King*, a project where shooting in virtual reality was central to the film's production. "It was our goal to sort of represent the whole world in VR, and then allow Matt [Reeves] to storyboard and shot-make as he went," said Chinlund. "We were breaking new ground and new tools the whole way, and it was just so exciting for us to see the power of the tool and its effectiveness in Matt's process, because I think it created a much more efficient relationship between

CONCEPT ART

the Art Department, Visual Effects, Storyboards, and Previs. Suddenly, we're all together working in the same space on the same box." When designing Selina Kyle's apartment, the team knew that the character's movements would need to be visibly tracked by Batman from an opposing rooftop—therefore they used the virtual reality tools to envision a space that feels aesthetically in line with the character yet encourages a flow of movement, from entering the apartment through to a street-level escape. However, designing a brand-new take on one of pop culture's most iconic locations is one thing—building a living, breathing Gotham City from the ground up is another, including everything from a working drainage system to take in the gallons upon gallons of Gotham City's rain, to an authentic and fully stocked bodega.

"More than color, texture was everything, and reflection," said James Chinlund. "The street is super messed up, and it actually took a tremendous amount of work to get it this way. The people who laid the asphalt, like, aren't used to making something so rough, but, for me the idea of the rain on the street at night and knowing that we'd be looking down the run of the backlot and feeling all that texture and displacement in the street was incredibly important—that everywhere you look, there're lumpy textures and rusty textures and things like that. And in this sort of noir dark lighting that we're working with, those things

really are the things that read." The use of light in *The Batman* was incredibly important to director Matt Reeves, and was baked into the developmental process from the very beginning. "Light has always been a critical and deeply emotional part of the image to me, and Greig obviously feels the same way. It is a huge part of our connection. We exchanged visual references, even while I was writing. And Greig is a master of light. His contribution to the way the film looks is monumental," recalled Reeves. "Down to the kind of lenses that we used. We used these wonderfully imperfect, anamorphic lenses that the rental house was like 'Are you sure you want these?' Greig's whole approach is about finding ways to bring texture into the overly clean digital image so it has a much more film-like quality. He'd even add water to the surface of the lenses in certain scenes, anything to make things more beautifully imperfect. And then, when it was all done, we printed everything onto film and scanned it back. We wanted the final film to look and feel like a neo-noir seventies thriller, in the vein of Gordon Willis's work in *Klute*, *The Godfather*, and *All the President's Men*."

In addition to the practical lighting that was already built into the sets, the filmmakers achieved a sense of realistic light by leaning into one of the most exciting new cinematography technologies available: LED volume capture. The use of blue- or green-screen techniques for shot composition has been industry standard since the 1930s, but not without some big limitations. For one, the sets were often a rather flat blanket of blue or green, giving little in the way of visual stimulus or a sense of what the eventual set might end up looking like, post-production. "I've worked a lot on green screen, and there's something good about having to use your imagination," said Zoë Kravitz, "but you're using a certain percentage of your energy, your attention, trying to picture what's out there." With the advent of LED screen technology, actors could actually see what they were meant to be reacting to, whether it was an otherworldly new planet, a terrifying monster's den, or, in the instance of *The Batman*, a sprawling cityscape—and with authentic lighting to boot. Kravitz continued, "Really looking out and seeing this beautiful light in the city, you're really able to lose yourself in the moment and not try and figure out what you're looking at. You and the person you're in the scene with are looking at the same thing, so you're in the same state. Me and Rob had this emotional and romantic scene on a roof, and to really have the light hitting our faces, looking out at the cityscape, it was a game changer." Director of photography Greig Fraser explains how it works: "If you drive into the middle of the desert, get out of your car at six P.M., and look around you, you are in a volume—because there's the sky, it's lit. There's the ground, it's bouncing light. You're in a volume of light—you just happen to be in a volume called the

atmosphere on planet earth. LED volume tries to mimic that situation, where you're surrounded by light on almost all sides. On the LED volume on *The Batman*, we tried to create a world where we created a volume of light that was Gotham in a number of different locations. You may not directly see a car headlight sweeping across Batman's face, or across Gordon's face, but you feel what is the conglomeration of all of those buildings together and the atmosphere illuminating our actors."

Rather than designing Gotham City's skyline after filming was completed, which may have been the case if using more traditional tools, the use of an LED volume required the city to be fully realized ahead of shoot. Tad Davis, visual effects art director, and Dan Lemmon, VFX supervisor, were able to work with the visual effects company ILM (Industrial Light & Magic) to combine the film's virtual reality technology with LED screens—something Greig Fraser considered to be a huge advantage. "James, ILM, and I basically all had an opportunity to design this city. You know, for me, it was very simple. I needed something that would do what I needed to do for light. From James's perspective, he needed something that would fulfill his vision of this incredible city that we're filming in. Then ILM needed to help marry those two ideas together, where they created content that was shootable, but also fulfilled James's vision and what I needed from the wall."

CONCEPT ART

BATMAN: YEAR ONE   David Mazzucchelli (pencils & inks)

ANATOMY OF A SCENE
THE DINER

Having followed The Riddler's meticulous series of clues, Batman, Gordon and the full might of Gotham City's Police Department are eventually led to a quiet diner positioned on the corner of Gotham City's downtown area. "The Diner is basically a straight riff on *Nighthawks* by Edward Hopper," recalled James Chinlund, production designer. "I love the idea of that glowing box of light in the middle of the dark space. Hopper really was a big inspiration for a lot of those things. We liked imagining that this diner sort of had a heyday and was part of a rosier time and then. *Nighthawks*, ever since I was a kid, was a huge image. I love the way the diner acts as a lamp in the center of a dark world."

Inside the eatery, The World's Greatest Detective and the GCPD discover a lone figure sitting at the counter, wearing plain clothes—nondescript if not for a familiar pair of glasses and a question mark that's been etched into the foam of his latte with a coffee stirrer: The Riddler himself, Edward Nashton. "One of the things that was important to me was to be a moment where you realized that when they capture The Riddler, they find him in this diner, and he's not wearing his mask, and so is that him?" said Matt Reeves. "I wanted the audience, when they see these glasses that he's wearing, to go 'Oh, those are the glasses." The impact of this reveal on the characters, and the audience, meant that filmmakers were required to design the diner set in a way that would accentuate the scene's action. "The amount of glass we have, and this big corner window—I love the idea of it being the fish tank," continued James Chinlund. "When we discover The Riddler, it seemed like the perfect opportunity to see him encased in glass in this glowing space, in this dark and rainy world. Through all this texture and rain and wetness and lenses, we'll have this amazing, glowing beacon in the middle of the dark."

Even after James had built the physical sets, we still had these digital environments, and I realized that I wanted to shot-make in the VR. I could go in with somebody who ran the game engine, and I put on the lenses and line up shots. It's a giant leap forward in being able to work in the virtual world, because for me everything is about standing in a space, looking through a lens, moving slightly to the left, looking slightly to the right, and going on a search.

MATT REEVES

VR TO SCREEN

140mm | Fdist:253.33cm | f/2.8 | 60/s | ISO100 | H:+0cm

140mm | Fdist:585.06cm | f/2.8 | 60/s | ISO100 | H:+0cm

105mm | Fdist:120.54cm | f/2.8 | 60/s | ISO100 | H:+0cm

VFX 3-D RENDERS AND FILM STILLS

105mm | Fdist:470.57cm | f/2.8 | 60/s | ISO100 | H.+0cm

105mm | Fdist:84.8cm | f/2.8 | 60/s | ISO100 | H.+0cm

190mm | Fdist:112.82cm | f/2.8 | 60/s | ISO100 | H.+0cm

VFX 3-D RENDERS AND FILM STILLS

CONCEPT ART

CONCEPT ART

CONCEPT ART

SQUARE GARDEN

ANATOMY OF A SCENE
THE GARDEN

Thousands have gathered inside Gotham Square Garden, the city's cavernous indoor arena, to rally for candidate Bella Reál on the mayoral election night. With a systemic history of corruption that has flowed through Gotham City's most powerful positions, Reál provides a powerful and honest pledge for change, and in turn a feeling of hope. "She is a grassroots organizer who is trying to make a difference in the city that she's born and raised in," describes Jayme Lawson, who stars as the young, inspirational politician. "She doesn't come from a wealthy background. She's really of the people and so, being somebody who was of the people, understanding the gripes within the city, being very hands on, she knows the real pains, the real conflicts in a way that all these politicians don't. She's deciding to try and shake things up and try to be an actual voice for the people."

The arena's attendees are initially oblivious to the events taking place outside, as The Riddler's true plan has been unveiled: the destruction of the seawall that protects Gotham City's downtown area. A series of timed explosions gives way to a tidal wave that floods its buildings and seriously endangers the lives of its citizens, causing even more people to huddle together inside Gotham Square Garden. The filmmaking team used a combination of locations (a dressed version of the inside of The O2 Arena in London, England, and the exterior of The James R. Thompson Center in Chicago) and visual effects to develop a brand new landmark for Gotham City, as well as a location that would house one of The Batman's most extraordinary and action-packed sequences. "This is an incredible special effects piece that was built by Dom Tuohy and his team," recalled production designer James Chinlund. "Dom had the great idea about building a piece of the seats of the arena to see the water cascading down. Matt's vision for the end of the movie was to see a massive wall of water coming through the city. Breaking that down into pieces that we can actually shoot and achieve was really, really tricky. Figuring out how to tell the story of the wave and the water was really a puzzle in and of itself."

CONCEPT ART

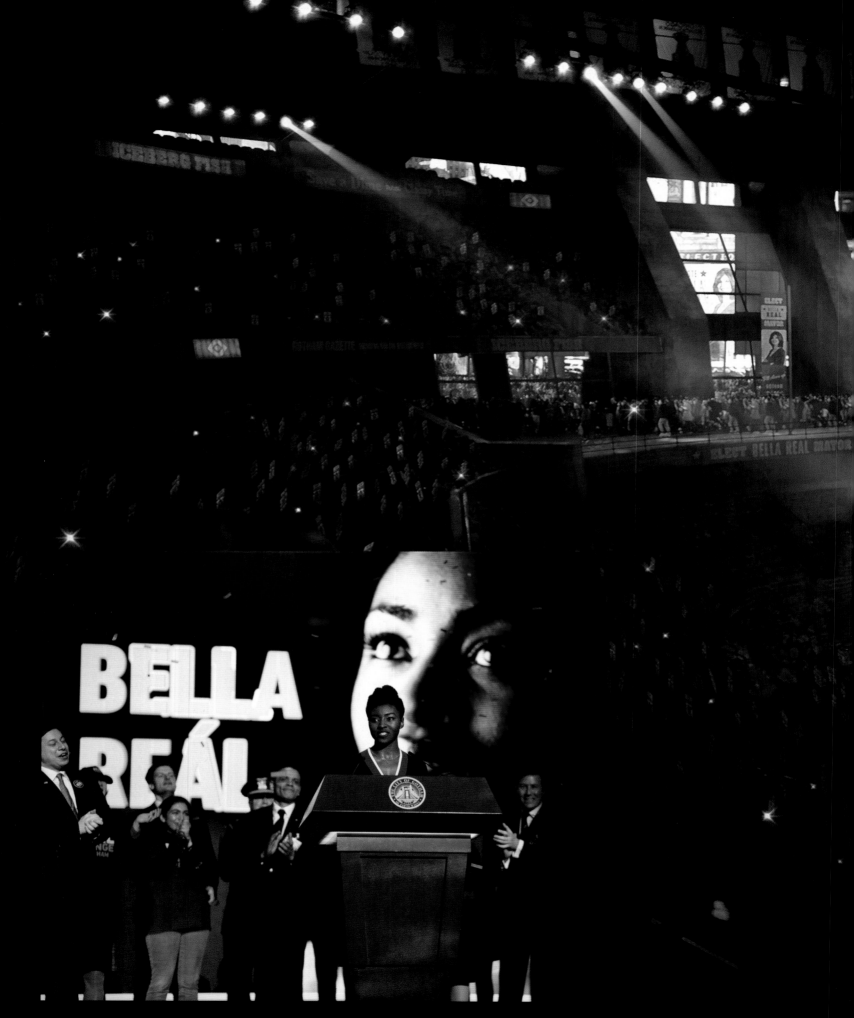

CONCEPT ART

CONCEPT ART

HOPE THE NEED FOR A HERO

"At the beginning of the story, he doesn't think that the city is capable of healing itself, and it's just on a downward spiral and he's just fighting a hopeless battle, which will end in defeat. I just always liked the idea at the end of him allowing himself to hope a little bit. It's probably the most painful thing that he has to do. It's much more painful than anything he's had to experience, because if you've closed yourself down to feeling anything, and all you wanna do is just go out and fight, if he allows himself to think that there is a possibility of positive change then you are set up to win. Then you

can feel the disappointment and failure of that as well, which I think he's trying to hide from as well. One of the first ideas I had about it was . . . I think a lot of the endings of Batman stories is that it ends with Batman believing that he's given hope to the city, and he thinks the symbol of Batman and what he's done throughout the story will hopefully inspire the city to have a more hopeful outlook, and create a brighter future. In this, I always imagined that he's so committed to darkness and nihilism that it's actually the city which opens up himself for his [hope]."

A graduate of Bournemouth University, **JAMES FIELD** has worked in the film industry since 2006. The International Winner of the Nickelodeon Writing Program 2016–17, Field has since divided his time between marketing and writing for film, television, and audio. He has worked as production liaison for both *The Batman* and *The Flash* which, as a lifelong Batman fan, is a dream come true. He lives in the UK with his partner and children

WITH THANKS Cassandra Casino, Alexandra Mason, Jesse Mesa, Katie MacKay, Shane Thompson, and Benjamin Harper

CONTRIBUTING ARTISTS Adam Brockbank, Ant Noble, Ash Thorp, Ben Last, Colie Wertz, Glyn Dillon, Jaime Jones, Joe Studzinski, Jon McCoy, Laura Dishington, Laurine Cornuejols, Mark Button, Matt Savage, Nathan Schroeder, Natasha Jones, Sam Williams, and Tina Charad

UNIT PHOTOGRAPHY Jonathan Olley, courtesy of Warner Bros.

CASE: CONCEPT ART

OPPOSITE: *BATMAN: YEAR ONE*
David Mazzucchelli (pencils & inks)

EDITOR Eric Klopfer
DESIGNER Liam Flanagan
MANAGING EDITOR Glenn Ramirez
PRODUCTION MANAGER Denise LaCongo

Library of Congress Control Number: 2021946849

ISBN: 978-1-4197-6210-9

Printed and bound in China
10 9 8 7 6 5 4 3 2

Abrams books are available at special discounts when purchased in quantity for premiums and promotions as well as fundraising or educational use. Special editions can also be created to specification. For details, contact specialsales@abramsbooks.com or the address below.

Abrams® is a registered trademark of Harry N. Abrams, Inc.

ABRAMS The Art of Books
195 Broadway, New York, NY 10007
abramsbooks.com